M000034809

PANDEMIC: THE BEGINNING

Pandemic Book One

CHRISTINE KERSEY

The characters and events portrayed in this book are fictitious. Any similarity to real persons, living or dead, is coincidental and not intended by the author.

Pandemic: The Beginning

Copyright © 2019 by Christine Kersey

All rights reserved

Cover by Novak Illustration

No part of this book may be reproduced, or stored in a retrieval system, or transmitted in any form or by any means, electronic, mechanical, photocopying, recording, or otherwise, without express written permission of the publisher.

Discover other exciting titles by Christine Kersey available through her official author website: ChristineKersey.com or through most online retailers.

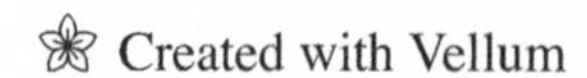

CHAPTER ONE

Jessica

The first sign that the world was about to come to an end was when Jessica's teenaged children informed her that Prom had been cancelled.

"Cancelled?" Jessica asked as she handed out bag lunches. "What on earth for?"

"Too many kids have the flu," Dylan, her fourteen-year-old said.

Jessica looked at Kayla for confirmation.

Sixteen and about to attend her first Prom, Kayla frowned. "It sucks."

"That's because you won't be able to make out with Ethan now." Dylan made kissing noises to emphasize his point.

Kayla swatted at him. "Stop it."

"Both of you stop it," Jessica said. "You're going to make me late for work." She loved her job as a dental hygienist, but now that she thought about it, a lot of patients had cancelled due to illness. Maybe her family should stay home for a day or two. Let whatever bug that was going around pass them by. None of them could afford to get sick.

Then she thought about Matt, her husband. He'd gone to work already. He was a software developer and Jessica knew he'd been stressed with all the work he had on his plate. Maybe she could convince him to work from home—something he did from time to time.

Sighing, she set her purse on the counter. "Okay. Family meeting."

"Wait," Dylan said. "We can't have a family meeting without Dad."

"I know, but this is different. He's not here and this seems like kind of an emergency."

"An emergency that there's no Prom?" Dylan rolled his eyes.

"It *is* an emergency," Kayla said.

"No," Jessica said. "Not because of Prom. Because of this flu. I've heard a few news reports that it's pretty nasty and it sounds like it's really going around. Maybe..." Was this really the best idea? "Maybe we should all kind of hunker down for a few days until it's—"

"Yes!" Dylan said, cutting Jessica off. "No school! Woo hoo!"

Kayla looked less certain. "What about, you know, missing all the stuff my teachers will be teaching?"

Dylan laughed. "You just don't want to miss seeing Ethan."

Kayla huffed out a protest, but Jessica knew what Dylan said was probably true.

"You can keep in touch with your friends," Jessica said. "Just not in person."

Kayla's lips compressed.

Jessica smiled. "Let me call Dad and see what he says."

Dylan had already set his lunch bag on the counter and dropped his backpack on the floor. "But we're not going to school today, right?"

Was Matt going to tell her she was being overly dramatic? Maybe, but in her gut she knew this was the right thing to do. "Yes. No school today."

"Woot, woot!" Dylan shouted as he pumped a fist in the air before racing for the stairs.

"Do you really think we could get sick?" Kayla asked, her forehead furrowed.

Though Jessica was concerned, she didn't want her kids to worry. "Not if we stay away from sick people."

"Mom," Kayla said as she rolled her eyes.

"Let me call Dad, okay?"

Kayla nodded, then she flopped onto the couch with her phone already in her hand.

Jessica went upstairs to the master bedroom and closed the door before calling her husband's cell. He answered on the second ring.

"What's up, honey? I'm about to head into a meeting."

Jessica pictured her husband—six feet tall, relatively fit, and still as handsome as the day she'd met him. "I was, uh, wondering if you could work from your home office today. And maybe tomorrow."

"What?" His tone showed he thought she was nuts. "Why would I do that?"

"Have any of your co-workers called in sick lately?"

He paused. "A few people have, yeah."

"More than normal?"

"I guess so, yeah."

"Honey, the kids' school cancelled Prom because so many kids have that flu that's going around. Just to be safe I'm, uh, I'm keeping them home for a few days. I'm going to stay home too."

"Really?" Shock was evident in his voice. "You never miss work."

"I know."

She heard noise in the background. It sounded like Matt had shifted the phone away from his mouth. "Hey," he said, "I've got to go. I'll call you after my meeting."

"All right, but think about it. Working from home, I mean."

"Okay. Bye."

Next, she called the dentist's office where she worked to let them know she wasn't coming in.

"Are you sick too?" Rochelle, her co-worker, asked.

"Too? Who else is sick?"

Rochelle named several others who worked there. Hearing the names of so many people she knew who were sick sent a beat of concern through her.

"No," Jessica said, "I'm not sick. Just trying to stay that way."

"Maybe you're on to something there."

Jessica thought about her co-worker and friend. Rochelle was sixteen weeks pregnant with her first baby. If she caught this flu, could it put her baby in jeopardy? "Maybe you ought to head home, Rochelle. Just in case."

Sighing heavily, she said, "I can't afford to take any more time off. You know how much time I took off when I was so sick at the beginning of my pregnancy. I used all my sick days."

Jessica bit her lip. "Just, I don't know, be safe. Okay?"

Rochelle chuckled. "I'm sure I'll be fine."

They disconnected and Jessica set her phone on her bedside table before turning on the news.

"...concerned about how quickly this flu is spreading," the news reporter was saying. Jessica turned up the volume. "The U.S. Centers for Disease Control and Prevention reports that this strain has resulted in higher than average fatalities and they remind people to take sanitary measures after being around other people. Wash your hands frequently, cover your mouth when you cough or sneeze, and if you or a family member has any symptoms, stay home for at least seventy-two hours after the symptoms have ended. This looks like a nasty one, folks."

The anchor went on to another story and Jessica shut off the TV, then used her phone to look up more information. She spent a good hour reading articles about the flu, each one making her concern notch up higher than the last.

She hoped Rochelle would change her mind and go home.

An image of her mom popped into her head. Recently diagnosed with breast cancer, her mom lived out of state. Alone. Jessica had already arranged to take time off the following week to fly out for a visit. She hadn't seen her mom in several months and wanted to spend time with her. She and her mom had always been close—being the only child of a single mother did that sometimes. It was important to her to be able to give her mom the support she needed.

Briefly wondering if this flu would affect her plans, Jessica shook her head. Surely by the next week the whole thing would have blown over. It had to.

"Mom?" Kayla said as she knocked.

"Come in, sweetie."

Kayla opened the door and sat on the bed. "What did Dad say?"

"He's in a meeting. He'll call me when he's done."

"But you told him about the flu?" She seemed much more worried than she'd been earlier.

"What's wrong, honey?"

"Nothing. I mean, I just..." She frowned. "I looked some stuff up. Just now? About the flu? Yeah. So. It sounds like it's not the regular flu."

That was the same conclusion Jessica was beginning to reach, but she wasn't about to share her worries. Not yet. Not when there wasn't a whole lot they could do about it. "People are working on it."

"What people?" Kayla asked. "What are they doing to fix it?"

Jessica struggled to come up with an answer.

Her phone rang, saving her from having to make something up. "It's Dad," she said as she looked at her phone.

Kayla frowned, then left the room.

CHAPTER 2

Matt

The moment Matt finished his meeting, he went to his cubicle and did some quick online research into the flu that Jessica had called him about. When she'd asked him if he would work from home, his first instinct had been to brush her off. He had a lot of work to do and he much preferred working in the office where he could chat with other developers. Three things made him reconsider. First, Jessica wasn't one to overreact, so the fact that she was staying home from work gave him pause. Especially since she was planning on taking time off to visit her mom the next week. Second, in the meeting he'd just gotten out of, half of the people who should have been there had called in sick. And finally, despite the fact that the media outlets were making a huge deal about this flu, he got the sense that maybe, for a change, they might not be exaggerating.

Decision made, he picked up his phone and called Jessica, his mind in task mode as he mentally listed all of the things they should do to prepare for the possibility that they would need to hunker down at home for an unspecified period of time.

"Hello?" Jessica said a moment later.

"Hi, babe."

Without greeting him, she said, "The news is saying this flu is pretty nasty. Some people have even died. More than is typical for a flu."

"I know."

"Are you going to come home?"

He could hear the worry in her voice. "Yes."

"You are?" Now hopeful disbelief.

Matt scrolled through the long list of software bugs he was assigned to fix and tried not to feel overwhelmed. His family's safety had to come first. "Don't sound so surprised."

"Okay," Jessica said with a laugh. "When are you leaving?"

Matt turned away from his computer screen and glanced toward his boss's office. "In a few minutes. I need to clear it with Dan first."

"At least traffic shouldn't be too heavy."

One side of his mouth quirked up. "True." He paused a beat. "I'm thinking of stopping by Costco on the way home to stock up on a few things. And fuel up my truck."

"Is that a good idea? I mean, what if sick people are

there? Besides, we have that freeze-dried stuff we bought a few years ago."

Several years earlier Matt had gotten interested in emergency preparedness so he and Jessica had splurged on a six-month supply of freeze-dried meals for their family of four. It still had more than twenty years of shelf life left, and it had been expensive. He really didn't want to use it if they didn't need to.

"I'd rather not dip into that," he said. "Not when I can go to the store and buy what we need."

Jessica was silent. "Okay. Just, please...be careful."

Matt laughed. "Oh, I will be."

They discussed what he should buy, and after he disconnected, he talked to his boss and got clearance to work from home for a while.

The drive from his job in Salt Lake City to the suburb where he lived in the southern part of Salt Lake County usually took thirty to forty minutes. Of course, that was during commute time in the late afternoons. Right now it was mid-morning so traffic was relatively light. Was that because of the time of day or because so many people had stayed home from work?

Shaking his head at the idea that enough people were sick that traffic would be affected, Matt took the exit that would take him to Costco. First, he went to their gas station, and after filling the regular tank on his truck with diesel fuel, he folded back a corner of the material that covered the bed of his truck before opening the cap on his auxiliary tank.

He and his family had a thirty-three foot fifth wheel RV, and when they'd looked for a truck to pull it with, they'd found one that already had a forty-gallon auxiliary tank installed. Matt loved the convenience of carrying over sixty gallons of fuel when pulling the RV. It really cut down on the need to pull the RV into gas stations not equipped to handle such a large rig. The only drawback was the cost. Dropping a couple hundred bucks on one fill-up was hard, but right now filling the auxiliary tank seemed like the prudent thing to do.

Once he'd finished filling both tanks, he parked his truck in the main parking lot. He was surprised at how busy Costco was at this time of day. Maybe it was always this busy—he'd never been there in the morning in the middle of the week. Besides, was Costco ever not busy?

Wanting a flatbed cart to haul his purchases, he looked around but didn't see any near the entrance. He had to walk back out to the parking lot to find one, and once he did, he went inside and started shopping.

Right away he noticed something unusual. Where the shelves typically had plenty of every item, now the supplies seemed to be depleted. And there were a lot of people with entire cases of canned goods in their shopping carts or on flatbed carts. More people getting cases of food than he'd ever seen before. It looked like everyone had the same idea he did. Ignoring the spark of alarm that lit inside his chest, he focused on loading whatever cases he could get onto his cart, as well as batteries and toilet paper. On one aisle, a woman began coughing. Everyone backed away from her, including Matt. He not only backed away, he went to a different aisle entirely.

Once he'd stacked all that would fit onto his cart, he made his way to the register. Long lines had formed—more like the lines he saw just before Christmas. And it was April.

Squashing the trepidation that kept pushing to the surface, he worked to stay patient until it was his turn to check out. Once he reached his truck, he began unloading everything into the back seat.

"Hey," a man said to him.

Matt turned to see what the guy wanted.

"I'll take that cart off of your hands when you're done."

Matt had other plans. "Thanks, but I have a few more things to get so I'll need to hang on to it."

The man scowled but walked away without incident.

Matt managed to fit everything inside the cab of the truck, and after locking the doors, he went back inside the store. To his surprise, it looked like the crowd had nearly doubled. And more than one person appeared to be sick.

Hurrying forward anyway, Matt avoided anyone who looked the slightest bit sick and loaded his cart with more canned goods and water, then he went to the area where vitamins and other health items were stocked. That section seemed less busy so he had no trouble getting what he wanted before adding boxes of protein shakes, protein bars, and two large first-aid kits. Then he noticed a shelf with three boxes of face masks. He set all of the boxes onto his stack of goods.

"You can't take all of those," a woman shouted as she ran up to him.

He glanced at the pricing label above the shelf, then turned to the woman. "Doesn't say there's a purchase limit."

She narrowed her eyes. "Don't you think someone else might want some?"

Matt stared at the woman, then decided it wasn't worth it to make a scene. He took one of the boxes off of his cart and handed it to her.

She snatched it from his hand. "I need one more."

Laughing at the nerve of the woman, Matt shook his head and walked away.

"Hey," she yelled.

Several people looked in their direction, but Matt ignored them and went to another aisle where he tucked the two boxes of face masks underneath other items on his cart so that they were no longer visible. Then he headed to the longer-than-ever lines at the register.

He made it to his truck without further incident, loading all of the items from this trip into the bed of his truck. Glad he had a cover over the bed of his truck to hide his purchases from prying eyes, he climbed behind the wheel. Hoping he hadn't forgotten anything, he left the parking lot and pointed his truck toward home. On the way, he passed a sporting goods store and decided to stock up on ammo for his .45 caliber pistol. While at the gun counter, he saw a 9mm that he thought was pretty sweet. Normally he wouldn't spend that kind of money without talking to Jessica, but he decided to buy it along with a rifle. He could always return them if Jessica objected. Since he had his Concealed Carry Permit, a background check wasn't necessary and he was able to walk out of the store with his newly purchased weapons.

On the drive home, Matt pictured the look on Jessica's face when he showed her all he'd bought. Was she going to laugh at him, think he was crazy, or be grateful?

Trying not to worry about that—most of what he'd bought they would eventually use anyway—he continued on his way.

CHAPTER 3

Jessica

What was taking Matt so long? It had been hours since he'd left his office. He should have already gotten home. Even with stopping at Costco.

Jessica tried not to worry, but her active imagination had Matt in a life-threatening car accident or some other awful situation.

"Mom," Dylan said, "I'm hungry."

Trying to push down her worries, Jessica told Dylan he could have an apple. Moments later she heard the deadbolt unlocking on the front door. Exhaling in relief, she hurried to greet Matt, sliding her arms around his waist.

"How'd it go?" she asked as she pulled away.

With a wry look, he tilted his head. "It was crazy there."

"Really? Crazier than normal?"

"I've never seen it this bad. Not even right before Christmas."

That concerned Jessica, because if that many people were as worried about this flu as she was, it had to be serious. "Were you able to get what you wanted?"

"Yeah."

"Good." They walked toward the kitchen. "By the way, make sure to wash your hands thoroughly."

Matt grimaced. "Good reminder. I think some of the people there were sick."

Startled, Jessica didn't say anything. No reason to get worked up over things they had no control over.

"Hey, Dad," Dylan said around a bite of apple.

"Hey, sport."

Matt turned on the water, then glanced at Jessica. "Can you move your car out of the garage? I want to back my truck in for us to unload."

Jessica's frowned. Matt never put his truck in the garage. Mostly because it was too long. "You won't fit."

He scrubbed his hands with soap. "I'll back in as far as I can. I, uh, I don't necessarily want the neighbors to see all of the stuff I bought."

"What'd you buy?" Dylan asked, his eyes wide.

Matt finished washing, then dried his hands on a towel. "Nothing exciting. Just lots of food. And I'll need your help to bring it in."

Dylan nodded. "Okay."

Jessica parked her car at the curb in front of the house and watched as Matt backed his truck into the garage.

Canned goods were stacked in the cab of the truck, and when he opened the gate on the back to reveal the rest of his purchases, she turned to him in shock. "How much did you spend?"

He looked a little sheepish. "I'm not sure you want to know. But I mostly bought stuff we'd use anyway." He grinned. "Now we won't have to go to the store for a while."

Jessica shook her head. "Yeah. Like, three or four years."

Dylan lifted a case of canned chili from the truck. "Where do you want me to put it?"

Matt turned to him with a smile. "Let's put everything in the basement storage room. And get your sister to help."

That brought a grin to Dylan's face. "Okay."

"Ask nicely," Jessica called after him. Then she faced Matt. "Do you really think you needed to buy so much?"

Matt lifted his shoulders in a shrug. "Who knows? But when I saw the purchasing frenzy and the shelves emptying out, I kind of panicked."

"Emptying out?" The shelves at Costco were never empty. Except for that one Christmas when a particular toy had been all the rage. But never food items.

"Yeah. A lady even yelled at me for taking the last boxes of face masks."

Jessica had trouble picturing a random stranger behaving that way. The people in their community were generally friendly. Especially when they were face to face with someone.

"Whoa," Kayla said with a smirk as she stepped into the garage and looked at the contents of the truck. "That's a lot of stuff, Dad." Face sobering, she looked at Matt. "Do you really think the flu is that serious?"

Jessica smiled. "I think your Dad went a little overboard."

Kayla's face smoothed out. "Yeah. And now we have to carry it all down to the basement."

"Yes, you do," Matt said. "So get busy."

Kayla rolled her eyes before hefting a case of canned green beans into her arms and heading into the house.

"I'm sorry," Matt said. "I didn't mean to go so crazy at the store." He chuckled. "You should know better than to send me alone."

Touching his arm, Jessica smiled. "No. I think what you bought is fine. I just…I said that to Kayla because I don't want her or Dylan to worry. This flu scare will probably pass like previous flu scares and we'll all be just fine."

"I hope so."

With that, they helped the kids carry the food down to the basement, although Jessica noticed Matt carrying several boxes of ammo into their bedroom. Curious what that was all about, she followed him.

"I didn't know they sold ammo at Costco," she said with a smirk.

He smiled as he put the boxes on a high shelf in their closet. "I stopped at a sporting goods store afterwards and decided to stock up."

She shook her head. "Are you done with your shopping spree now?"

He laughed. "Yeah. I think we're good. Unless you want to risk going out?"

"No. That's what online shopping is for."

His face got serious. "That's actually not a bad idea."

"What do you mean?"

"We ought to see if there's anything else we should have on hand. You know, in case of an emergency."

Jessica agreed, and once the truck had been completely unloaded and moved back into the driveway, she and Matt sat in front of the computer and pulled up Amazon. They ordered a number of items to add to their emergency stores, including a solar hand crank radio/flashlight, four portable water purifier straws, and four bug-out bags, each one providing seventy-two hours of supplies.

"In two days we'll be ready for the end of the world," Matt said with a grin.

Jessica forced a smile, hoping that in two days they would be laughing at themselves.

CHAPTER 4

Jessica

"Mom!" Kayla said the next afternoon as she raced into the living room, her tone nearing hysteria.

Jessica set down the book she'd been reading and leapt to her feet. "What's wrong?"

"Brooke's mom," Kayla said as tears filled her eyes.

Jessica pictured Kayla's best friend Brooke. Tall and slender with long auburn hair, she was a fixture around their house. Jessica didn't know Brooke's mom well, but she'd always been friendly. "What happened?"

"She died." Kayla's face crumpled as tears streamed down her face. "Brooke's mom *died*."

Jessica drew Kayla into her arms as shockwaves cascaded over her. "What?" She slowly pulled away from Kayla, her mind racing. "When? How?"

"Today."

"Oh my goodness! What happened?"

"She was fine last night, but she woke up feeling sick." Kayla's voice shook as she spoke. "Brooke's dad took her mom to the hospital, but she died, Mom. She's *dead*." Tears rolled down Kayla's cheeks.

Astonished, and rather alarmed, Jessica needed to know more. "What did she have? Do they know?"

Kayla stared at Jessica as stark panic washed over her face. "The flu. It was the flu."

Jessica's mouth fell open. It was shocking that someone could be fine one day and dead the next. From a virus.

"Mom. What if Brooke gets the flu? I mean, she was exposed to it, right?" Fresh tears filled Kayla's eyes. "What if Brooke dies too?"

Jessica didn't want to point out that any of them could catch the deadly flu. And she had no words of reassurance to give Kayla.

"What's going on?" Matt asked as he came into the room. He'd risen early and had worked from his home office all day.

After hearing about Brooke's mother, Jessica was doubly glad Matt had agreed to work from home.

"Brooke's mom passed away." Jessica's voice was surprisingly calm. "From the flu."

Matt went to Kayla and wrapped her in a hug. She lay her head against his shoulder and sobbed. As he comforted her, his gaze met Jessica's. Jessica read the worry in his eyes as clearly as if he'd said the words out loud.

"I feel like I should do something," Kayla said as she stepped away from Matt, her face streaked with tears.

"What would you like to do?" Jessica asked.

"I don't know. Bring her and her dad something to eat?"

Jessica's gaze slid to Matt, who subtly shook his head, then Jessica looked at Kayla. "That's very sweet of you, but under the circumstances I don't think it would be a good idea to go over there."

Deep creases formed on Kayla's forehead. "Right. Of course."

Relieved that Kayla understood, Jessica gave her another hug and murmured, "I love you, sweetheart."

"I love you too," Kayla whispered, then she turned and headed toward her room.

Later that evening, the four of them gathered in the family room to watch the local news. Jessica sat on the couch beside Matt, and Dylan sprawled on the floor. Kayla, however, sat on the edge of the recliner, her back ramrod straight as the four of them waited for the broadcast to begin. Moments later it did. The first announcement was that the schools in multiple school districts in the state, including theirs, would be closed until further notice. It had been decided that since so many kids were sick, it would be best to keep everyone home.

"No school?" Dylan said as he looked at Jessica and Matt. "Whoa."

"Guess you guys won't be missing anything by being home," Matt said with a sardonic grin.

"This is crazy," Kayla said, her gaze glued to the TV.

"Crazy awesome," Dylan said with an ear to ear smile.

"I know it seems great," Jessica said, "but remember what's behind it. People are getting sick." She glanced at Kayla. "Sick enough to die."

Dylan's smile vanished. "Yeah. I know."

During the broadcast, Jessica kept thinking about Rochelle. After they'd spoken the day before, had she decided to stay home today?

When the news was over, Jessica went into her bedroom and called her.

"Hello?" a gravelly voice said.

Had Jessica gotten the wrong number? The voice that answered sounded much deeper than Rochelle's. Maybe it was her husband? "Is Rochelle there?"

"It's me, Jess."

Unease rattled through her. "Are you sick?"

"I should have listened to you yesterday. I should have gone home. I feel like death warmed over."

Oh no. "Have you been to the doctor?"

"I have an appointment in the morning."

That was something, at least. "I'm so sorry you're sick."

"You and me both."

They didn't talk long, and after they hung up, Jessica called her mom.

"Hi, sweetie," her mom said, her voice cheerful. "How are you?"

Half expecting to learn that her mom had caught the flu —after all, with the cancer treatment, her immune system had been weakened—when her mom sounded like her normal happy self, Jessica quietly exhaled in relief. "I'm good. I wanted to see how *you're* doing."

"Same old, same old. I spent most of the day working on my new quilt. It's coming along beautifully, Jessica. I can hardly wait to show it to you when you're here next week."

Thrilled her mom was doing as well as possible, Jessica sat back and enjoyed their chat, still hopeful that she would be able to make the trip.

That night after Jessica and Matt got in bed, they turned on the news. As expected, the main topic of discussion was the flu that was sweeping the country and even the world. They listened in quiet horror as the anchor calmly announced that the fatality rate was climbing and that it was becoming common to catch the flu and die in a single day.

"That's what happened to Brooke's mom," Jessica said barely above a whisper, as if saying it any louder would bring the same fate to their house. Could the same thing happen to Rochelle? Appalled by the thought, she decided she would call her first thing in the morning to check on her.

Matt leaned over and kissed her on the lips. "I'm glad you convinced me to work from home."

Pushing aside her worries, she put her arms around him and lay her head on his chest as a feeling of safety washed over her. "I'm glad you agreed."

They listened as the news anchor talked to a representative from the CDC.

"Turn that up," Jessica said as she straightened. Matt complied, and Jessica breathed a sigh of relief when the woman from the CDC said that it appeared that the incubation period from being exposed to the virus to when symptoms appeared was twenty-four hours.

"It's been longer than that since any of us have been around other people," Jessica said. She turned to look at Matt. "Does that mean we're safe?"

He grimaced. "I hope so."

CHAPTER 5

Matt

"Rochelle's not answering her phone," Jessica said to Matt the next morning.

Working in his office, he turned to her with confusion. "Who?"

"Rochelle? From work?"

He still didn't know what she was talking about. "Okay."

She dragged her hands through her hair. "When I called her last night she was sick. She was going to the doctor this morning, but she's not answering her phone."

Knowing Brooke's mother had died from the flu, Matt understood why Jessica was worried. Still, he didn't want her to jump to conclusions. "Maybe she was in with the doctor when you called."

Jessica's face relaxed a little. "Maybe." She pulled her

phone out of her pocket. "I'll text her and ask her to call me." She gave him a quick kiss. "Sorry to bother you."

He smiled. "You never bother me."

She returned his smile. "I'll let you get back to work."

Later that morning the doorbell rang. Ready for a break, Matt got to the door in time to see the UPS driver walking away from the packages he'd left on the porch. Watching the man through sidelights beside the front door, when the driver lifted his hand to his mouth and had a coughing fit, Matt recoiled. He couldn't bring the packages inside. The virus could be all over them.

"Are those our packages from Amazon?" Jessica asked.

The kids were right behind her.

"Who was that?" Dylan asked.

Frowning, Matt turned to them. "Yes, it's our packages. But I think the delivery guy was sick. He was coughing up a lung."

"You can't bring them in," Kayla said. "I mean, what if the delivery guy has the virus? Could we get it?" Concern filled her eyes. "I don't want to get sick."

Matt stepped away from the still-closed front door and went to Kayla before pulling her into a hug. He knew she was thinking of Brooke and her family. Besides, he agreed. "We'll do everything we can to stay healthy." He stepped back. "Any ideas?" He glanced at Dylan to include him in the question.

Dylan, who usually made fun of his sister at every opportunity, was uncharacteristically helpful. "What if we leave them on the porch for a few hours? Won't the virus die?"

Kayla didn't look convinced, but Matt smiled. "That's actually a good idea, Dylan."

Dylan grinned under the compliment.

"How long does it take for the virus to die?" Kayla asked, her eyes tight with worry.

"I'm not sure," Matt said. "Let me look it up." He pulled his phone out of his pocket and Googled the question. Moments later he frowned as he looked at Kayla. "This virus can live on hard surfaces for up to twenty-four hours."

Jessica looked thoughtful. "What if we spray some disinfectant on the boxes?"

"Do you really think that would kill the virus?" Dylan asked.

Looking grim, Jessica shrugged. "I don't know. Or we can wait until tomorrow to bring them in."

"And risk someone stealing them off of our porch?" Matt shook his head. They had important supplies in those boxes. He wasn't about to risk someone taking them. The way things were going, he was becoming more convinced by the minute that all the things he'd bought two days earlier plus the items on their porch would become vital. Especially as the news reported increasing fatality rates.

Jessica sighed, clearly stressed by all that was happening. "What do you want to do?"

That's when Matt got an idea. "Wait here. I'll be right

back." He went out to their RV which was stored in the side yard, took a small box out of the storage area, and came back into the house. He held up the box of disposable gloves that he used when emptying the RV's waste tanks. "Problem solved."

"What are you gonna do?" Dylan asked, his face bright with interest.

Matt put on a pair of the blue disposable gloves and a face mask, then he went to the laundry room where the cleaning supplies were stored. He took out a spray bottle of disinfectant and carried it back to where his family waited.

"I got this," he said with a grin. He went into the garage and pressed the opener. Once the garage had rumbled open, he went to the front porch, sprayed a generous mist of disinfectant over the boxes that sat on the porch, then carried them one by one—careful to hold the boxes away from his body—into the garage. When he was done, he tossed the gloves in the trash, closed the garage, and went inside where he washed his hands with soapy water before putting the face mask aside and turning to his family with a triumphant smile. "We'll leave them in the garage for at least twenty-four hours."

"Dad," Dylan said with an ear-splitting grin, "you're a genius."

"That was pretty smart," Kayla said.

Jessica wrapped her arms around him. "I knew I married you for more than your good looks."

Enjoying the accolades from his family, he laughed.

CHAPTER 6

Jessica

Jessica hadn't heard back from Rochelle. She'd made several other attempts throughout the day to call her, but each time the call had gone straight to voice mail. Concerned, but not knowing what to do, she hoped Rochelle would finally get in touch with her and tell her she was okay.

That evening as Jessica was making dinner, Kayla came into the kitchen. "Mom?"

"Hi, honey." She put the casserole in the oven and set the timer for thirty minutes.

"Mom. I don't know what to do."

She turned to face her. "About what?"

Kayla sighed. "Brooke keeps asking me if I can come over."

"No." The words left Jessica's mouth without thought.

Eyes widening at Jessica's tone, Kayla said, "I know I

can't go over there, but what should I tell her? I mean, her mom died and now her dad's sick."

Thoughts of Rochelle, sick the night before, filled her mind. "Oh no."

Her expression must have broadcast her worry, because tears filled Kayla's eyes. "He's going to die, isn't he?"

Jessica rushed to Kayla and put her arms around her. "Not necessarily, sweetheart. Not everyone who gets sick dies." She desperately hoped that was right.

Kayla stepped back, her eyes wet. "Yes, they do. I read it online."

Had the fatality rate climbed higher? "Where did you read that?"

Kayla took her phone out of her pocket, tapped something into the screen, then showed it to Jessica, who read the headline: *Fatality rate skyrockets to ninety-five percent*.

Terror slammed through her. Pressing a hand to her chest, she found it hard to catch her breath. She had to talk to Matt, had to discuss what to do. But first she needed to comfort Kayla.

She put an arm around Kayla's shoulder as they both stared at the ominous words. "I'm so sorry, sweetheart."

"Everyone's going to die, aren't they? Even us."

Jessica met Kayla's gaze. "No, no, no. That's why we've quarantined ourselves. To stay healthy. To stay alive."

Kayla's forehead creased like she didn't quite believe her. "I'm gonna call Brooke."

Jessica loved Kayla's compassion. "Good idea. She needs all the support you can give her."

The moment Kayla cleared the room, Jessica hustled into Matt's office. It looked like he was deep into coding, and though she didn't want to interrupt him when he was in the flow, this couldn't wait. "I have some news."

He spun his chair to face her, his expression guarded. "Bad news?"

Jessica frowned. "That's all we seem to have lately."

"What is it?"

"Brooke's dad is sick now."

Matt's forehead furrowed. "Oh no."

"Yeah. Evidently the fatality rate is now ninety-five percent."

"What?"

She gave him the web address for the site Kayla had shown her and they looked it up together. With a more thorough read, the news was even worse than Jessica had at first realized. Not only had the fatality rate skyrocketed, but the virus was spreading extremely fast.

Matt turned to her, his expression sober. "You realize what this means, don't you?"

A million thoughts flew through Jessica's mind but she didn't want to give voice to a single one of them. Still, she had to know what Matt was thinking. "What?"

"This thing could lead to collapse."

She knew what he was saying but she didn't want to accept it. "What kind of collapse? What do you mean?"

His face was grim. "Total societal collapse."

"From the flu? No." She shook her head in denial. "No. That can't happen, Matt. Why are you saying that?"

"Think about it, Jess." He held up his hand and touched a finger. "If enough people die, who's going to deliver food to the stores?" He touched a second finger and then a third. "Who's going to run the water treatment facilities? The sewage treatment facilities?" He touched a fourth. "Who's going to keep the electrical grid going?"

Panic, powerful and swift, crashed over her. How could a little flu bug lead to all of that? "But not everyone is getting sick."

Matt gazed at her. "Do you think anyone who's healthy is going to want to go to work?" He gestured to the programming code on his computer screen to emphasize his point. "I'm not."

"Can't they work from home too?"

He tilted his head like he didn't want to point out the obvious because it was such a horrible truth but he had no choice. "There are only so many people who know how to run the utility companies and it's unlikely all of them will survive this. And those who do probably have to be at the facility to do their job." He frowned. "Then there are the truck drivers who deliver food to the stores. Do you think those who survive would want to be out among the sick? And you know stores only have a few days' worth of food in stock." Matt shook his head, his lips lifting in a grim smile. "Good thing we stocked up when we did. If there's so much as a single bottle of ketchup on the shelves at this point, I'd be shocked."

As it dawned on Jessica how this had the potential to turn into an absolute nightmare, she felt her face pale. "How bad do you think it's going to get?" Her voice was soft, like if she didn't say it very loud, it might not happen.

Matt grimaced. "We haven't even discussed law enforcement."

"What do you mean?"

"Those officers have families of their own. Don't you think they'll want to protect them from all the chaos? Sure, there might be a few out there trying to uphold the law, but how long do you think that will last?"

"You're really scaring me, Matt."

He placed his hand on her knee. "We need to be prepared for the worst." He gazed at her. "That includes the kids."

Jessica thought about her kids and how their lives were about to change. If they survived the flu, that is.

The thought horrified her.

The timer went off in the kitchen. Glad for an excuse to end this disturbing conversation, she stood. "Dinner's ready."

CHAPTER 7

Matt

Matt followed Jessica into the kitchen, his mind on all the horrible things he'd told her. He deeply hoped society would make it through, but he feared a collapse was inevitable.

"Mom, Dad," Dylan said from the family room. "Come see this." His tone was laced with unease.

"What is it?" Matt asked, walking into the family room and standing behind the couch where Dylan was sitting.

Dylan pointed to the TV and turned up the volume. Matt's eyes went to the flat screen mounted on the wall. It was breaking news. The anchor, a woman who was on every night, was calmly sharing the latest information on the flu with a video showing people, some of them wearing earloop masks, fighting over nearly empty shelves at grocery stores. The video changed from one location to another, covering cities in multiple states, but the story was the same over and over.

"Hospitals are full," the anchor stated, "so if you have symptoms, the best place for you and your loved ones is at home."

"They don't want people to spread it," Dylan said, then he looked at Matt. "Right?"

Matt set a hand on Dylan's shoulder. "Yeah. I think you're right."

"If anyone in your home has died, authorities ask that you mark your house by painting a red X on your front door or putting a red sheet of paper in your front window. They also ask that you wrap any dead bodies in a sheet until the authorities can collect them."

Repelled at the idea, Matt stared at the TV.

"Dinner's ready," Jessica called from the nearby kitchen.

Matt turned and looked at her. Anxiety was etched on her face.

"It's ready," she said again, as if feeding their family was the only thing she could handle just then.

"Go get your sister," Matt told Dylan. Once Dylan had left the room, Matt turned off the TV then went into the kitchen. "You saw the news?"

Jessica nodded, but kept her gaze focused on the salad she was tossing. "Uh-huh."

A few minutes later the four of them sat around the dining room table, each of them lost in their own thoughts.

"Brooke said her dad…" Kayla's voice broke. "She said

he looks like her mom did right before she died." Tears overflowed Kayla's lashes. "She's going to be an orphan." Kayla glanced at Dylan. "She doesn't even have any brothers or sisters. It's just her."

Jessica leapt to her feet and raced to Kayla's side, wrapping her arms around her. "I'm so sorry, sweetheart."

Matt watched helplessly as Kayla sobbed and Jessica comforted her. After a moment he went to them and put his arms around them both. After several minutes Kayla calmed and they went back to their seats, but no one seemed to be hungry. Even Dylan, who usually ate whatever was placed in front of him.

Matt didn't want to add to everyone's distress, but he needed to have a serious talk with his family. "Family meeting after dinner." His tone was grim.

Everyone looked at him with furrowed brows.

Compressing his lips, he met all of their gazes. "I know you might not be all that hungry right now, but we need to eat while we can."

"Matt," Jessica started, but he shook his head. He wasn't ready to discuss this until after dinner.

A soft sigh slipped from Jessica's lips, but he ignored it and focused on finishing every bite on his plate.

After the dinner dishes were cleaned up, the family gathered in the family room, their faces anxious. Jessica sat next to Matt on the love seat, Kayla and Dylan sat on the couch.

Matt looked at the faces of his children. Kayla was barely old enough to drive and Dylan was just starting to get zits. Still so young, but it was his responsibility to make sure they were as prepared as possible. "As you've seen for yourselves, things have changed. Drastically."

Tears filled Kayla's eyes, but Matt could tell she was doing her best to keep her emotions in check.

"We've done a few things to prepare," he said, "but there are things you need to know." He turned to Jessica. He knew she had to be thinking about their conversation before dinner. Would it be too much to share his fears with his children? Maybe so. He could give them hints without going into too much detail though. Enough to prepare them without scaring them to death.

"What?" Dylan asked.

Matt turned his attention back to the kids. "If things don't change, if people keep," he looked at Kayla, "dying...well, things are going to get rough."

"I already know," Dylan said.

Matt narrowed his eyes. "What do you mean?"

"I've seen The Walking Dead, Dad. I know what can happen."

"This isn't like that."

Dylan snorted a laugh. "Right. No zombies."

"It's not funny," Kayla said as she gave her brother a shove.

He turned to her, his face somber and his voice gentle. "I know."

Kayla's lips lifted in a tiny smile, like she knew her brother hadn't meant any harm.

Deciding to let the kids steer the conversation, Matt asked, "What do you think is going to happen, Dylan?"

Dylan glanced at Kayla, then he faced Matt and Jessica. "A lot of people are going to die." He bit his lip. "Maybe even us."

"We're doing everything we can to make sure that doesn't happen," Matt assured him.

"I know," he said, "but it's possible."

Matt couldn't argue with that. Still, he wanted to reassure him. "As you know, we've self-quarantined and we'll do our best to stay safe until this flu has run its course."

"Will it?" Kayla asked. "Run its course, I mean."

This wasn't something Matt could be sure of, but he drew on past history. "There have been pandemics before and they always come to an end. Eventually."

"But how long will it take?" Kayla persisted.

Matt turned to Jessica as if she would have an answer. She looked back at him, then she pulled out her phone.

"Let's look it up," she said, her voice businesslike. She read her screen then looked at him and the kids. "Past pandemics have taken a few weeks to several months to run their course."

"Are you saying we have to stay locked in our house for *months*?" Kayla asked, her face incredulous.

"Let's hope not," Matt said, glad that was her main concern.

"That's not the biggest problem," Dylan said.

And here we go.

Kayla turned to her brother. "Okay. What's the biggest

problem? Because I don't think I can stand staring at your face for *months*."

Dylan's eyebrows shot up like he was offended, then he shook his head like his sister was an idiot. "You'll be lucky if that's your biggest problem." He smiled and ran his fingers through his hair. "Besides, I'm one handsome guy."

Kayla snorted and turned away. "Yeah, right."

Dylan looked slightly hurt. "I am."

"Yes you are," Jessica said.

Dylan grinned.

Glad his kids still had a sense of humor, Matt smiled. "Back to the subject at hand." He looked at the kids. "Tell me what *you* think we're in for."

"Worst case scenario," Dylan said, "no food, no water, no power, no cops."

That about covers it.

Kayla's gaze shot to Matt, her eyes wide. "Is that true?"

"We don't know if that's what will happen," Jessica said before Matt had a chance to respond.

"But what if it does?" Kayla's forehead was creased like she had no doubt that's *exactly* what would happen.

"That's why we're having this meeting," Matt said with a glance at Jessica, who stared at him like she hoped he wouldn't go there. He turned to Kayla and Dylan. "That's why I wanted you to eat your dinner whether you were hungry at that moment or not. We have a good supply of food and we have a decent supply of water, but I think it would be a good idea to fill all of our pitchers with water as well. Plus, I'll fill the RV's fresh water tank."

Kayla's phone chimed a text. She glanced at the screen, then her eyes went wide and she cried, "No!"

"What's wrong?" Matt asked.

Kayla looked at him, her face filled with shock. "Brooke's dad died."

CHAPTER 8

Jessica

Jessica had feared that Brooke's father wouldn't make it, that it was inevitable he would die, but she'd held out hope nonetheless. Now, that hope was gone. She stood from the love seat and went to Kayla, wrapping her arms around her as Kayla sobbed.

"Brooke's an orphan," Kayla moaned. "An actual orphan. Her mom and dad are dead. We're all gonna die!" The hysteria in her voice rose with each sentence and all Jessica could do was hold her and murmur that everything would be all right.

"No it won't," Kayla said as she pushed Jessica away. "Nothing will ever be all right. Not anymore."

Kayla was completely right. Jessica didn't see any point in arguing against what they all knew to be true. All she could do was stay by Kayla's side with her arm around her shoulder.

"I don't want to talk anymore," Kayla whispered.

"I think we've done enough talking for one night," Matt said, much to Jessica's relief.

They put on a favorite movie, a comedy from years past, but there was very little laughter as the four of them stared at the TV.

The movie seemed so pointless. People were dying. How could they sit there watching such an inane show?

Holding back a sigh, Jessica excused herself and went into her bedroom and called her mother.

"Hi, honey," her mom said, her voice sounding less cheerful than it had when she'd spoken to her last. In fact, it sounded like it was well on the way to how Rochelle's voice had sounded.

"How are you?"

"Not good, baby."

Tense with worry, Jessica asked, "What's wrong?"

"I don't know. Earlier today I started to feel unwell. Scratchy throat, aches and pains. That kind of thing."

Dread spiked within her. "Do you have a fever?"

"I don't think so. I mean, I've been so chilled."

Jessica thought of both of Brooke's parents dying, of Rochelle being sick and now not answering her phone, of the fatality rate skyrocketing to ninety-five percent. Tears flooded her eyes and a sob leapt up her throat.

"It's okay, baby," her mom said. "I'm sure I'll be just fine."

Had her mom not seen the news, or was she trying to

placate her? Either way, the thought of losing her mom tore her apart.

"Jessica? Are you there?"

"Yes," she croaked out.

"Oh, sweetheart. Don't cry. I'll see you in a few days and we'll have a great time."

Jessica didn't have the heart to tell her mom that there was no way she would get on an airplane, trapped in a metal tube with recirculated air and potentially sick people. Besides, she knew the chance that her mother would survive was extremely low. Especially with how weak the cancer had made her. "I love you, Mom."

"I know, sweet girl. I love you too. I always have." Her mom sniffled. "You're my heart."

Her mom knew she was going to die.

A fresh sob welled up inside Jessica.

She needed to get herself under control, needed to take this time to talk to her mom.

Breathing deeply, she gathered her emotions. "Tell me about that quilt you've been working on. The one you sent me a picture of."

"The one with the flowers?"

Jessica nodded, overcome with emotion once again. "Yes," she whispered.

"Oh, it's coming along beautifully."

Jessica listened as her mother spoke, soaking up every word, every syllable, listening to her mom talk until she said, "You know, honey, I'm feeling really tired. I'm going to bed now. Let's...let's talk in the morning."

Knowing full well that by morning her mom would most likely be dead, for a moment Jessica couldn't catch her breath. It felt as if a band had wrapped around her chest and was compressing, compressing, compressing.

"Good night, my love," her mom said, sounding exhausted.

Rallying, Jessica said, "Good night, Mom. I love you."

"I love you too. Sleep well."

With that, all was silent. Her mom had disconnected the call. That was when Jessica let the sobs overtake her, bathing her face in tears.

CHAPTER 9

Jessica

After lying awake most of the night, Jessica got up before the sun, tiptoed out of her bedroom, went into the family room, and dialed her mother.

The phone rang and rang.

It was no more than she'd expected, although she'd held onto the hope that her mother would answer. She left a message, asking her mom to call her the moment she woke, then climbed back in bed.

"No answer?" Matt asked. She'd told him and the kids about her mom the night before in an attempt to prepare them for the worst.

Silently, she shook her head.

He wrapped her in his arms. "I'm so sorry."

Savoring the warmth of his body curled around hers, she turned her thoughts to him and their children. A burst of gratitude that they were healthy swept over her. And she knew, somehow, that her mom was at peace.

The next afternoon as Jessica was in the basement storage room organizing all the food Matt had bought, Dylan came bursting into the room. "Mom," he said, his voice breathless.

Knowing it would be bad news, Jessica dreaded asking, but did anyway. "What is it, honey?"

"No airplanes are allowed to fly."

She tilted her head in question. "What are you talking about?"

"They said so on the news. Just now."

She followed Dylan up the stairs and into the family room where the news was broadcasting. A camera was panning a huge airport where airplanes were parked everywhere.

"Still no word on when planes will be back in the air," the news anchor said, "but unnamed sources say all planes will be grounded indefinitely due to the spread of what is now being called the bird flu."

"What do airplanes have to do with the flu?" Dylan asked.

"Well, if someone is sick and gets on the plane, they can pass the flu on to the other passengers who can then pass it on to everyone they come into contact with. Before you know it, it's spread all over the world."

"Don't you think it's already spread all over the world? I mean, it's been going on for a week and people have been flying all over the world the whole time."

Dylan was right and Jessica knew it. Grounding the planes might help slow the spread, but stopping it now was impossible. "I don't know," she said, not wanting to alarm Dylan unnecessarily.

The news anchor turned to her guest, a man from the World Health Organization, who basically said the same thing that Dylan had.

"See?" Dylan said with a proud smile.

"Yep." She ruffled his hair. "You're one smart kid."

"I'm not a kid anymore, Mom."

Jessica was beginning to realize that. Because with the way the world was crashing all around them, he and Kayla were going to have to grow up fast. "I know, sweetheart," she said, then she went to Matt's office to tell him what she'd just learned.

His door was closed and she could hear talking. Not wanting to interrupt if he was in a conference call, she slowly twisted the doorknob and opened the door a crack, but when she saw that he was watching the news on his monitor, she walked in and closed the door behind her.

He turned at her approach. "I just heard about the planes."

"Might be a little too late to stop this thing." She frowned as she pulled a chair up to Matt's desk so they could watch the broadcast together. "I've been doing inventory on all the food and supplies in the storage room."

Matt turned the volume down and faced her. "And? How are we looking?"

For a change she had good news. "Pretty good." She grinned. "You did awesome with your shopping."

One side of his mouth quirked up. "That's a first."

She leaned forward and kissed him on the mouth. "I love you."

"I love you too." Then he gazed at her. "We're going to get through this. All four of us."

As scared as she was, and as sad as she was about her mom, she couldn't allow herself to think anything but positive thoughts. "As long as we stick together, we'll be fine."

Matt nodded. "Tell me more about our inventory."

Glad to talk about something tangible, Jessica said, "With what you bought the other day, plus that six-month supply of freeze-dried food we bought a few years ago, we're actually in great shape."

"That's fantastic."

Both their gazes went to the computer monitor, which was still showing the news broadcast. It was five o'clock. Time for an update.

Matt turned up the volume.

A man they'd never seen on that news station sat in the anchor's chair, his expression stoic.

"He's new," Jessica said as a sense of foreboding washed over her.

"Good evening," the man said. "My name is Kevin Burns. I am a producer, not a reporter, but today I am filling Amy Hunter's shoes, so to speak, because she is..." The man's chin quivered slightly, but he held it together. "Amy Hunter passed away this morning."

Jessica shook her head. Another illness, another death.

Kevin Burns stared into the camera. "Last night Amy came down with the bird flu, and..." Frowning, he looked at the surface of his desk before facing the camera again. "That is how quickly this virus kills." He visibly swallowed. "I have to be honest with you, folks. Amy is not the first person at this news station to...to die...from the bird flu." He paused. "I fear she won't be the last."

Kevin was silent for several seconds. "We will continue broadcasting and bringing you the news as long as possible —we can get by on a skeleton crew if needed, but..." His jaw worked. "We've lost a lot of our people and many others are too scared to come in." A grim smile tugged up the corners of his mouth. "I don't blame them. But, like I said, we are here to keep you apprised of what is happening in our community and country and around the world and we will do that for as long as we are able."

Pounding on their front door startled Jessica. Matt stood and headed out of the office. Jessica followed close behind.

CHAPTER 10

Matt

Hurrying through the family room, Matt held up a hand to Dylan and Kayla, who were standing near the front door with worried expressions. The blinds were down, covering the two long narrow windows on either side of the front door so Matt couldn't see who it was. "I'll handle this."

They nodded and stepped out of the way. Matt lifted a slat on the blinds, peeking out through one of the sidelights.

"Who is it?" Jessica whispered from beside him.

He turned and frowned. "Our neighbor. Jack Peters."

Pounding sounded again, putting Matt on edge.

"What do you think he wants?" Jessica asked as Dylan and Kayla huddled around her.

He shook his head. "No idea." Matt pulled the blinds up and Jack came into view.

Jack's gaze shifted to Matt. Wild-eyed, Jack practically pressed his face against the glass. "I need help."

"What's going on?" Matt asked as alarm flared inside him. Jack and his family lived two doors down. Matt didn't know him well, just well enough to chat with him if they both happened to be outside at the same time. Jack was Matt's age—late thirties—and married. He and his wife had two school-aged children.

"They're all sick," Jack said as tears filled his eyes. "All of 'em."

Alarm turned to empathy. "Your family?"

Jack nodded. "We need help."

Matt had no idea what he could possibly do to help them. "Have you called your doctor?" The answer sounded lame even to him. Jack's family would most likely die. Calling the doctor would be a waste of energy.

"Yes," Jack said, his face nearly crumpling. "The doctor's office just had a recording to call 911, but when I did, I got a busy signal." Panic swelled in Jack's eyes. "I called and called and called, but no one's answering."

Fresh alarm swelled inside Matt but he tamped it down. "I'm sorry, Jack."

Jack's eyes widened. "Sorry?! Sorry doesn't help."

Baffled as to what to do, Matt shook his head. "There's nothing I can do."

Jack turned away from the window and battered the door with both fists. "Open the damn door!"

Kayla screamed.

"Don't open it," Jessica shouted.

Turning to his family and holding up a hand, Matt gave them a look that said *I've got this*. Then he looked back at Jack, whose palms were now flattened against the glass. Speaking calmly yet firmly, Matt said, "You know I can't open the door, Jack. Now, go home to your family and make them comfortable." An image of his own family, sick and dying, flashed through his head and he almost lost his cool. But he couldn't think about that. He had to keep his composure, had to get Jack away from his front door.

"I just..." Jack began, then he lowered his head as tears dripped down his face. His head lifted and he looked at Matt, pleading in his eyes. "Do you have any Tylenol? To ease their pain?"

They had lots of Tylenol, and Matt was completely willing to give some to Jack, but he couldn't open the door. He couldn't chance exposing his family to the virus.

"Tell you what," Matt said, "come back in half an hour and I'll leave some Tylenol on our porch."

Relief flooded Jack's face. "Thank you."

Glad he could do something that might help but wouldn't endanger his family, Matt watched Jack turn around and make his way down the walkway to the sidewalk. When he was out of sight, Matt turned to face his family.

They stared at him in silence.

"That really freaked me out," Kayla finally said, her voice nearly shaking.

"Me too," Dylan added.

Matt's eyes sought out Jessica, who smiled softly at him

before placing her hand on his arm. “You’re a good man, Matt Bronson.”

Matt smiled at her.

“Why did you tell him to wait half an hour?” Dylan asked.

Looking at his son, Matt said, “Jack didn’t look sick, but in case he is, I wanted to give the air by the door time to clear out.”

Dylan nodded. “Makes sense.”

“Is that enough time?” Jessica asked.

Matt had no idea.

“You can’t open the front door,” Kayla said. “What if the virus is still in the air and it gets in the house?”

“Wait,” Dylan said. All eyes shifted to him. “What if you go out through the garage? Then you won’t need to open the front door.”

“You’re brilliant, son.”

Dylan beamed.

“I’ll get a bottle of Tylenol,” Jessica said, then she went into the kitchen. Moments later she was back holding a small baggie with some pills in it. “I don’t think we should give away an entire bottle.” She grimaced and held up the bag. “This should be enough to hold them for a while.”

Matt knew what she was saying. Jack’s family would be dead within hours. They didn’t need an entire bottle of pills.

Leaning forward, Matt kissed Jessica on the lips, then he took the baggie from her. He put on a face mask, then walked to the door that led to the garage. “I’ll be back in a minute.”

He opened the door and went into the garage, then went to the man-door that led to the backyard, opening it and stepping outside. The sun shone brightly, belying the turmoil that lay beneath its bright orb.

Matt tilted his face toward the sun, soaking up its warmth, then he turned to the gate that led to the front of the house, reaching for the latch. He hesitated. He hadn't been out front in days. What would he find?

Drawing in a lungful of air, he braced himself, exhaled, then opened the gate and stepped through, the baggie of Tylenol in his hand and the mask covering his nose and mouth.

Nothing. That's what he saw. Nothing and no one. All was silent. Eerily silent. It was a spring afternoon. Children should have been outside playing, riding bikes. People should have been mowing their lawns, working in their yards. Instead, not a soul could be seen.

Frowning, Matt strode across his driveway and toward the walkway that led to his front door.

Movement caught his eye.

It was Jack. He'd been hiding around the corner of Matt's house, but now he was barreling toward Matt, his eyes wild with fear.

Sheer panic engulfed Matt. Flinging the baggie of pills in Jack's direction, Matt spun on his heel and bolted back in the direction he'd come.

"Wait!" Jack screamed from ten feet behind him, pure hysteria in his voice. "I need your help."

Ignoring Jack's plea, Matt propelled himself through the

open gate, then slammed it closed behind him. A second later Jack crashed into the vinyl gate, rattling it on its hinges.

Not waiting to see if Jack would open the gate and come through, Matt burst through the man-door, shutting it behind him with a bang before turning the deadbolt. Chest heaving and heart hammering against his ribs, Matt bent over, placing his hands on his knees. He didn't know how much his family had witnessed, but he didn't want them to see the terror in his eyes, so he took a moment to catch his breath and gather his emotions.

CHAPTER 11

Jessica

Jessica admitted it. She'd been terrified to have Matt go outside and into their own front yard. What was this world coming to? A week ago she wouldn't have thought twice about it. But now? Now, everything had changed. Friends and family were dropping like flies and she and Matt had to do all within their power to keep their family safe.

She stood beside the sidelight, anxious to know what was happening. All of a sudden Jack raced across the lawn in the direction Matt was coming from. Panic, stark and clear, shot through her and she flew to the front window to see what was happening. The kids were right on her heels.

"What's going on?" Kayla asked, her voice constricted with fear.

The three of them stood at the front window, but they couldn't see a thing. Not with the way the house was situated. Jack had run to their left, toward the garage side of the house. Jessica had heard him yelling that he needed help, but that was all she'd been able to see. "Dad needs us."

"What should we do?" Dylan asked, his eyes wide.

Jessica thought about the gun and ammo she'd seen Matt bring in on the day of his shopping spree. Matt had shown her where he was storing his weapons.

Not taking the time to answer Dylan, Jessica ran to the closet in the master bedroom and quickly found a gun. Then she grabbed a loaded magazine before dashing to the garage. She pressed her ear against the door, but after hearing nothing, she opened the door, her gaze darting around the space until she saw Matt, bent forward with his hands on his knees.

"Matt," she said.

He straightened and spun around, his eyes wide as he took off his face mask. "Jess, what are you doing?"

Seeing that he was alone and that the door leading to the backyard was locked, she took the two steps down into the garage, and with the gun pointed at the floor and the magazine in her other hand, she walked toward Matt. "Are you okay?"

"Yeah."

"I saw Jack running." She stopped beside Matt and held out the gun for him to take. "I was worried so I brought you this."

He stared at the gun in her hand like it was a foreign object, then he gazed at her before finally taking it and the magazine from her.

Not sure what she expected him to do, she stood there watching him, waiting for some kind of guidance. When he didn't say anything, she asked, "What happened out there?"

With a look of disbelief, he slowly shook his head. "Jack's gone stark raving mad."

At that moment, pounding sounded on the man-door.

Jessica let out a scream, her heart in her throat. "Is that him?"

Matt's gaze shot to the door, then he shoved the magazine into the gun. "Yeah."

He seemed rather calm, which helped to settle Jessica's nerves.

Matt walked to the door and shouted, "Jack! Calm down."

"Open the door," Jack yelled. "Open it right now."

Matt shook his head. "No can do, man. The Tylenol is out front. Grab it, then get off my property."

"Or what?" Jack said, his voice shaky yet defiant.

Matt racked the slide, the sound loud and clear. "Or I *will* shoot you."

Jessica stared at Matt, her eyes wide with shock and fear. Would Matt really do that? But one look at his face and she believed him wholeheartedly.

There was silence on the other side of the door.

"Do you think he left?" she whispered.

Matt looked at her, his expression serious. "Don't know, but I'm not gonna open the door to find out."

They stood there for at least two minutes before Matt lowered the gun.

"Let's go inside," he said, tucking the gun into the back of his waistband.

Jessica was more than happy to comply. She led the way, and the moment they stepped into the house, the kids began asking what had happened.

Matt came into the house, locking the door behind him, then, without answering the kids, he strode to the front room. Jessica and the kids followed him. When they caught up with him, Jessica looked over his shoulder as he peered out the window, and to her great relief, she saw Jack trudging down the sidewalk, away from their house.

Exhaling audibly, Jessica felt her shoulders begin to relax. "He's gone," she said.

"But will he come back?" Matt muttered.

She didn't want to consider that, but she knew Matt was right. After all, Jack had hidden in the shadows waiting for Matt to appear. Who knew what he was capable of? His family was dying. He had to be desperate.

Matt stepped away from the window and turned to Jessica and the kids. "I'm going to board up the windows by the front door."

Anything to keep them safe. "Good idea."

"I want to help," Dylan said.

"What happened out there?" Kayla asked. "I mean, we saw Jack running, Dad. Did he touch you?"

Matt smiled and shook his head. "No, sweetie. I made it back into the garage before he caught up with me."

This was surreal. Their neighbor had chased Matt down

and Matt had threatened to shoot him if he didn't leave. All because of a virus. A *deadly* virus.

Blinking to clear her mind, Jessica forced a smile but she felt like a fraud. She'd never been so worried and so terrified in her life. She liked to be in control, and right now she wasn't. Not in any way, shape, or form. And she was pretty sure she wouldn't be for a long, long time.

While Matt and Dylan went out to the garage to get scraps of wood along with a hammer and nails, Jessica thought about Jack's comment that no one was answering 911. Curious if he was exaggerating, she went into her bedroom and closed the door, then dialed 911. A busy signal sounded. Just as Jack had said. Frowning, Jessica tried again. Same result. Then she tried one more time. Busy.

What was happening? Why was no one answering? Was help even available? Was everyone home with their families? Or were so many people sick or dead that there simply weren't enough people to help?

The thought that there was no one to call in an emergency made Jessica extremely nervous. What if someone got hurt? Or what if someone tried to break in? What if Jack came back with a gun of his own and shot his way into their house? There was no one to call for help. It was all up to them.

With shaking hands, Jessica tucked her phone into her back pocket.

They were on their own.

CHAPTER 12

Matt

"We'll have to cut this down to a narrower size," Matt said as he hefted a large sheet of plywood. It was left over from a woodworking project he'd recently completed. He'd almost tossed it, but now he was glad he hadn't.

Dylan helped him move some things around in the garage so he could wheel his table saw into a space where he could work. A few minutes later they had two long, narrow sheets of plywood that would fit perfectly over the sidelights.

"Grab the hammer," he said to Dylan. Then, with the two sections of wood in his hands, he turned to go into the house.

"Dad," Dylan said, his tone stopping Matt in his tracks.

"Yeah?" He lowered his arms so that the edge of the wood rested on the ground, then he turned to Dylan.

With his hands holding the hammer and a box of nails, Dylan gestured to Matt's back with his chin. "Why do you have a gun in the back of your pants?"

He'd forgotten that was there, but after what had happened with Jack, he had every intention of keeping it handy.

"Uh," he said, "just in case."

Dylan grinned. "Can I have a gun?"

"No," Matt said without thinking. Then he realized he should probably take some time to teach both Dylan and Kayla how to use his guns. At a minimum, he needed to review gun safety.

At the look of disappointment on Dylan's face, he smiled. "You can't have a gun, but I'll show you how to use it. Okay?"

Dylan's face lit up. "Okay."

He thought about Jessica. She wasn't going to be happy about what he'd just promised.

Not able to worry about that just then, he picked up the wood and carried it into the house, then he and Dylan nailed the boards into place.

It looked eerie and kind of creepy to have wood covering the glass, but if that's what it took to keep deranged neighbors and anyone else who might wish to do them harm from getting inside—or at least slowing any intruders down—then the boards would stay.

"Dad's gonna show me how to use a gun," Dylan said.

Matt turned around to see who he was telling, hoping it

was Kayla so he would have a chance to talk to Jessica about it first, but no luck.

"Oh really?" Jessica said.

"Yeah," Dylan said, excitement in his voice. "Then I might get a gun of my own."

Jessica's eyes widened as she stared at Matt. "Can I talk to you?"

"Yeah. Sure. Let me put my tools away and then we can go into my office."

After putting the hammer and box of nails in the garage, Matt turned to Dylan. "Let me know if anyone comes to the door, but don't open it."

Dylan rolled his eyes. "Of course not, Dad."

"Thanks." Matt went into his office with Jessica. She closed the door and sat in his desk chair. He sat in the other chair. "The kids need to know how to use guns safely."

"That's not what I want to talk to you about."

That surprised him. "Okay."

She scraped a hand through her hair. "I called 911—"

"What for?" he asked, cutting her off. Would he get in trouble for threatening to shoot Jack?

"I wanted to see if they would answer."

That's when he remembered Jack telling them that no one had picked up when he'd called 911. "Oh. And?"

She clutched her hands together. "I tried three separate times and each time all I got was a busy signal."

That was deeply concerning. "Let's try again. Maybe it'll be working now."

She nodded, clearly eager to be proven wrong.

Matt pulled his phone out of his pocket, dialed 911, then put the phone on speaker. A busy signal filled the silence.

Jessica cupped her face with her hands. "See?"

Quietly sighing, Matt put his phone back in his pocket.

Jessica dropped her hands to her lap. "There's no one to help us. If someone gets hurt, we're on our own. If the house catches fire, we're on our own." Her voice became louder with each sentence. "If someone wants to hurt us, Matt..." Her eyes were bracketed with terror. "We'll be on our own."

Knowing they had no one to turn to in a true emergency made Matt feel cut off. And after what had happened with Jack, he was wary to reach out to his neighbors.

Suddenly it didn't seem so crazy to teach his fourteen-year-old son how to use a handgun.

"What are we going to do?" Jessica asked as her hands twisted together in her lap. "I mean, what if Jack comes back with a gun and forces his way inside?"

"That's not going to happen."

"You don't know that."

His shoulders slumped. "No. I don't." Then he straightened in his seat. "But you don't know that he will, so let's not assume the worst."

She sighed. "Fine."

When they finished speaking, Matt stood, prepared to discuss gun safety with his family.

"Are you ready?" Jessica asked as she stood beside him.

He nodded, not liking that he was being forced to teach

his fourteen-year-old son and sixteen-year-old daughter how to use a gun in self-defense. Against neighbors.

"Yeah," he murmured.

Side by side, he and Jessica walked into the family room, but when they crossed the threshold, they found Kayla and Dylan sitting on the couch in the family room with Kayla holding the remote and frantically changing channels.

"What's going on?" Matt asked.

Kayla turned and looked at him, her eyes wide. "None of the news channels are on."

"What?" He held out his hand and she gave him the remote. He went to their favorite local channel, but it was showing a sitcom. "That's weird." For the last two days, it seemed as if the only thing all the news channels were broadcasting was information about the bird flu. "Maybe people were tired of hearing about the flu."

Then he went to Fox News. Vertical colored bars covered the screen. They were off the air.

Stunned to see something he'd never expected to see on a twenty-four hour news station, he felt his mouth fall open as he turned to Jessica, who looked just as shocked as he felt.

"It's the beginning of the end, isn't it?" she whispered.

He didn't want to acknowledge it, but he couldn't deny the obvious. "Yeah."

CHAPTER 13

Jessica

Jessica was having a hard time accepting what Matt had just acknowledged.

The end had come. The end to all she'd known. The end to safety and security. The end to her easy life, to the comforts she'd always taken for granted. The end to society.

The end to life as she knew it.

"What's happening?" Kayla asked, her voice gushing fear.

With her throat filling with a rapidly growing knot, Jessica couldn't speak. Instead, she placed what she hoped was a comforting hand on Kayla's shoulder.

"The newscasters aren't on," Matt said, stating the obvious.

"They're all dead, right, Dad?" Dylan asked, his eyes tight with distress.

Matt had a grim look on his face. "I don't know. They probably just don't have enough people to run things."

"No," Kayla said. "They're all dead."

With the matter-of-fact way Kayla had said that, Jessica didn't know how to reply. Because she knew her daughter was right.

The doorbell rang.

They all froze.

Jessica's gaze shot to Matt, whose eyes were wide as he stared at the front door. With the sidelights boarded up, they had no way to see who was on the porch. There was no peephole.

"Who do you think it is?" Kayla frantically whispered as she stood from the couch.

An image of their desperate neighbor, Jack, flew into Jessica's mind. It had only been a few hours since he'd been there. Had his family died? Had he come back with a gun? Ready to kill them all?

Terror wound its way up Jessica's throat. She could hardly breathe.

A knock sounded. Not the pounding that Jack had done earlier, but a soft, hesitant tapping.

That almost made it worse. Like he was trying to draw them out.

Matt moved toward the front door.

"No," Jessica whisper-screamed. What if Jack had a gun? What if he shot through the door and hit Matt? *Killed* Matt?

Matt stopped and turned to her. He softly sighed before

walking the rest of the way to the door. "Who is it?" he called through the door.

Jessica's gaze was riveted to the door.

"Brooke," a soft voice answered.

It wasn't Jack. Slumping in relief, Jessica shifted her gaze to Matt, who turned and looked at her with a question in his eyes.

"She might be infected," Dylan said.

"She's an orphan," Kayla said, her voice hitching like she was trying to hold back tears.

Jessica regarded her daughter, trying to imagine what it would be like if Kayla was left completely alone and went to Brooke's family for shelter. What if they turned her away?

The thought broke her heart.

Then she thought about her mom and Rochelle. Dead. So many dead. They couldn't leave Brooke out on her own.

"We have to help her," Jessica heard herself say.

Matt stared at her, then he turned to the door. "Are you sick?"

"No," Brooke said.

"Come to the living room window." He walked to the large window and opened the blinds. Jessica and the kids followed. Brooke came into view. Her hair was disheveled, she looked exhausted, and she had a backpack slung over her shoulders. But she didn't look sick—good color in her face, eyes clear. She just looked like someone who had been through hell.

"Are you alone?" Matt asked.

Brooke glanced to the side as a German Shepherd appeared next to her. "Cleo's with me."

"Okay. Hold on a minute."

She nodded again.

"You're not going to let her in, are you?" Dylan asked, his face panic-stricken. "If she's infected she'll kill us all."

Matt's gaze went from Jessica to Dylan to Kayla. "I don't think she's sick."

"You can't know that," Dylan said, his voice tense.

"I have an idea," he said, then he turned to Kayla. "Gather some blankets and a pillow."

Kayla's eyebrows bunched, but she nodded, then left the room. A few moments later she was back with what he'd requested.

"Follow me," he said before turning and walking out to the garage.

All three of them followed him, watching as he took an air mattress from a shelf, blew it up, then spread blankets on it.

"What if she and Cleo stay in here until the incubation period has passed? If Brooke's healthy, she and Cleo can come in." He looked at each of them, clearly wanting their agreement.

"That's a good idea," Jessica said.

"Yes," Kayla said as a relieved smile lit her face.

"Yeah," Dylan added. "I guess that would be okay."

"Let me put some food and water out there for them," Jessica said. Hurrying into the kitchen, she gathered what she had in mind. Once she'd set the items in the garage, she nodded to Matt.

He unlocked the man-door that led to the backyard, opened it, peered outside, then closed it, leaving it unlocked.

The four of them went back into the house, locked the door from the garage to the house, and walked to the front window.

Brooke and Cleo stood where they'd left them.

"You and Cleo go into the garage through the backyard door and lock it behind you," Matt said. "Knock on the door that leads to the house when you're safely inside the garage."

A tentative smile lifted Brooke's lips. She nodded. "Okay."

The four of them hustled to the door that led to the garage. A knock sounded on that door.

"I'm here," Brooke said.

"Is the door to the backyard locked?" Matt asked.

"Yes."

"Okay. Do you have food for Cleo?"

"Yes."

"Okay, here's what we're going to do." Then he explained their plan. "You and Cleo should have what you need to get you through until tomorrow evening."

"Thank you," she said through the door.

Jessica could hear tears in her voice and wanted nothing more than to gather her daughter's best friend into her arms and tell her everything would be okay.

She only hoped it would be, and that Brooke wasn't carrying the virus that had killed both of her parents.

CHAPTER 14

Matt

Matt tossed and turned all night, his mind on Brooke. Had he endangered his family by letting her in? True, it was just the garage, but if she was sick, the virus would be all over the garage, all over their things.

It had been a mistake, he was sure of it. But he couldn't leave her on her own. She was just a teenaged girl. An orphan. Letting her in had been the right thing to do. Besides, she might be perfectly healthy. Although she had been around two people who had died from the virus so she had to have been exposed.

All night long his thoughts went like that. Back and forth, back and forth. Didn't matter though. She and her dog were in their garage and that couldn't be changed. They would just have to see what happened. If worse came to worse, they would disinfect the entire space. After waiting a few days to let all the virus hopefully die, that is.

"Are you awake?" Jessica murmured beside him in their bed.

He smiled in the darkness. "How could you tell?"

"Normally when you sleep you're dead to the world, not constantly moving."

Facing her, he propped himself up on one elbow. He was able to make out her face in the dim light that trickled in through the partially opened blinds from the street lamp outside. "Sorry if I woke you."

She reached out and stroked his face. "You didn't. I was already awake."

"What's got you up?"

"I was thinking about Brooke. I mean, what if she's sick?"

He sighed. "Exactly what I was thinking."

She sat up. "Let's check on her. Through the door, I mean."

"Yeah. Good idea."

Together, they walked toward the kitchen where the door to the garage was. To their surprise, they found Kayla sitting on the floor, her back against the door.

"What's going on?" Jessica asked, alarm in her voice. "You didn't open the door, did you?"

The light over the kitchen sink was on, casting enough light to help Matt see Kayla roll her eyes.

"Of course not. I'm talking to her through the door." She glanced at the phone in her hands. "And sometimes texting." She softly smiled. "I have to talk kind of loud for her to hear me through the door and I didn't want to wake you guys up." Her eyebrows tugged together. "Did I wake you up?"

Matt shook his head. "We were already awake. We came to check on Brooke." He sat on the floor beside Kayla. Jessica sat beside him. "How's she doing?" He glanced toward the door as he spoke.

"Not good," Kayla said, her face crumpling into tears.

Matt couldn't help it. He recoiled. "She's sick?"

"What?" Kayla asked. "No! No. She's not sick. She's just really sad."

Exhaling in relief, when he considered what it would feel like to lose his entire family, his heart lurched.

"Can we let her in?" Kayla asked, her eyes filled with empathy.

"Not yet, sweetheart," Jessica said, which made Matt glad. He didn't want to be the bad guy. "We have to wait twenty-four hours from when she got here."

"I know," Kayla said. "I just…I feel so bad for her."

Loud sobbing from the other side of the door interrupted their conversation. Without thinking, Matt reached out and placed his hand on the door. "We're here, Brooke. We're here for you."

"I know, Mr. Bronson," she said, her voice breaking. "I'm sorry to be a…a bother."

"You're not a bother," Jessica said loudly. "We're glad we can help you. We just, we have to make sure you're not sick."

"I know."

"What's going on?" Dylan asked as he stumbled into the room rubbing his eyes. "I heard voices."

"We're talking to Brooke," Jessica said.

Matt loved his family dearly, and he loved that they felt like a team, that they were all there together in the middle of the night, all thinking about the same thing. Well, maybe Dylan hadn't been thinking about Brooke, but still, he was there with them.

"Is she sick?" Dylan asked around a yawn as he sank onto the floor near Matt.

Matt ruffled Dylan's hair. "I don't think so."

"The sun's coming up," Jessica said as she stood. "I'll get breakfast started."

"What about Brooke?" Kayla asked.

"I'm sorry, sweetie," Matt said. "She'll have to make do with the food Mom put out there."

Kayla frowned but she didn't argue.

As the day went on, Matt checked on Brooke from time to time, speaking to her through the door. Kayla pretty much camped out beside the door.

As the twenty-four hour mark came, Matt took Jessica aside. "One of us needs to go into the garage and evaluate whether Brooke is sick or not."

"I'll go," Jessica said without hesitation.

He shook his head. "I should do it."

Jessica narrowed her eyes. "Why?" Then she smirked. "Do you have some special medical knowledge that I'm unaware of?"

He chuckled. "You know I don't."

She laughed. "So, why you?"

He shrugged. "Because I'm the one who let her in."

She shook her head. "No. That's not a good reason. Besides, I think she'd feel more comfortable with me."

Matt couldn't disagree with that. "All right. Fine. But you need to wear a mask and gloves. Just to be safe."

Jessica nodded. "Of course."

CHAPTER 15

Jessica

Why had she volunteered to face a possibly sick person? Someone who could unwittingly kill her with a virus?

Jessica tightened the mask around her nose and mouth as she tamped down her fear.

She didn't want anyone in her family to take this risk, but she knew she would be careful.

She put on goggles before pulling on a pair of gloves.

"Ready?" Matt asked as he stood beside her in the kitchen. Kayla and Dylan were there as well, their faces filled with anxiety.

"Yeah," she said, her voice muffled.

"Okay," he said before walking toward the garage door.

Jessica followed, her body tense with uncertainty. What if Brooke was sick? All day she'd claimed to be feeling fine, so maybe she was. Besides, if she'd gotten sick, chances were she would be on the verge of dying.

That thought shook Jessica, and when Matt turned the deadbolt on the garage door, Jessica froze. Could she handle seeing a dead body? In her own garage? Especially one that belonged to her daughter's best friend?

Chest tight, Jessica held up a hand to Matt, signaling for him to wait.

"Do you want me to do it?" he asked, his forehead creased.

She didn't want him to have to face this either. Besides, Brooke wasn't dead. She'd just said she felt fine. "No," she said, coming out of her paralysis. "I'm ready." She really wasn't, but this was her world now and she would have to deal with whatever was placed in front of her.

"Please stand back," Matt said through the door.

"Okay," Brooke answered.

Matt turned the doorknob and gently pulled the door open, staying away from the opening. Jessica's gaze went to the cavernous space beyond the door. She didn't see Brooke. Was she hiding because she was sick? What if she was lying in wait for Jessica, ready to infect her? Jessica had never heard reports of how those who were infected behaved once they were sick. Would Brooke go crazy on Jessica?

With a glance at Matt, Jessica stepped over the threshold. The moment she cleared the doorway, Matt closed the door behind her. Thankful he hadn't locked the door, Jessica looked around the space.

"Brooke?" she called out.

"I'm over here," a soft voice said.

Jessica looked to her left. That's when she saw her. Brooke stood near the door that led to the backyard, holding Cleo by the leash. Cleo leapt and panted, her tail wagging with delight, but Brooke's shoulders were slumped and her face was incredibly sad.

Empathy flooded Jessica. She took a step in Brooke's direction. From where Jessica stood, Brooke didn't look sick. "How are you feeling? I mean, are you sick?"

Brooke shook her head, then she burst into tears.

That did it. Jessica walked swiftly toward Brooke with her arms outstretched. Brooke dropped Cleo's leash and raced into Jessica's arms, sobbing against her shoulder. Jessica had questions for her, but for now she just held her. With Brooke in her arms, Jessica noted that Brooke wasn't feverish. That was a very good sign.

Cleo pranced around them, clearly excited at being around a new person.

Finally, when Brooke's tears began to slow, she drew away from Jessica and Jessica got a closer look. Besides having a tear-soaked face, Brooke looked fine.

"Let's go inside," Jessica said with a soft smile.

Brooke nodded, then followed Jessica to the door.

When they stepped inside, Jessica noticed that her family was standing back quite a distance, watching them enter, their eyes glued to Brooke.

"She's not sick," Jessica stated.

At that, everyone's faces relaxed and Kayla went to Brooke and hugged her.

Cleo had been at their house before, so she was familiar with the members of the Bronson family, so when Dylan called her over, she went to him happily

"I made space for you in my room," Kayla said to Brooke with a warm smile. The girls went down the hall to Kayla's room, Cleo on their heels.

"Are you sure she's not sick?" Dylan asked. "I mean, how can you know for sure?"

In reality, the only way to know was to wait and see, but it had been over twenty-four hours since Brooke had been around the virus and she was healthy. Hopefully that was good enough.

"Nothing's sure anymore," Matt said, saving Jessica from having to explain. "But if she's not sick yet, I don't think she'll get sick."

"I'm going to get dinner started," Jessica said as she took off her mask, goggles, and gloves, then turned to walk into the kitchen.

That evening at dinner, with Brooke eating with them—something she did quite often—it almost felt like a normal night.

"I wonder what happened to Jack," Kayla said as she picked at the food on her plate.

Jessica thought about their neighbor and the terrifying interaction Matt had had with him, the way Jack had hidden around the corner of the house waiting for Matt to appear. "I don't know." Although she was fairly certain

Jack's family had died. Had he as well? "Maybe we should check with our neighbors," she said. "See who's still healthy."

"Too dangerous," Matt said.

"Well," Dylan said with a smirk, "we could, you know, call them."

Matt smiled. "Yeah. Except I don't have their phone numbers. Do you?"

They'd lived in their house for two years, but in that time they'd only gotten to know a few neighbors, and that was mostly when they happened to be outside at the same time as them.

"No," Dylan said with a frown.

"Wait," Jessica said, "Cathy down the street gave me her number once." She got up from the table and dug around in the kitchen junk drawer before coming up with a slip of paper with a name and number. She held it up in triumph and smiled at Matt, who had a look of anticipation on his face, like he was eager to hear what was going on outside the four walls of their home—even if it was just a few doors down.

Jessica listened as the phone rang. And rang and rang. Was Cathy still alive? The thought that no one they knew still lived was eerie and unsettling.

"Hello?" a soft voice answered.

"Cathy?" Jessica said as her gaze shot to Matt, who was listening intently.

"Yes. Who is this?"

Jessica put the phone on speaker and set it on the table

so everyone could listen. “It’s Jessica Bronson. Your neighbor?”

A slight pause. “Oh yes. How…how are you? How’s your, uh, your family?”

Cathy was obviously wondering if Jessica was sick and if her family was alive. Relieved to be able to report that they were all well, Jessica opened her mouth to speak. But then wondered if Cathy would have news just as good. It seemed unlikely. Still, Jessica had to know what others were experiencing.

“We’re good,” she finally said. “All of us.” Then she glanced at Brooke, who met her gaze before casting her eyes toward the tabletop.

“I’m…I’m so glad to hear that,” Cathy said, her voice hitching.

“What about you?”

A quiet sob filled the space. “Dean didn’t make it.”

Jessica pictured Cathy’s husband. He’d always been so friendly and willing to help. The thought of him dying hit her hard. She swallowed the tears that threatened. “I’m so sorry, Cathy.”

“The rest of us are okay though.”

Cathy had two teenaged boys. Jessica was thrilled that they were there for Cathy. She couldn’t imagine how horrific it would be to lose her entire family. Then she thought about Brooke, who *had* lost her entire family. It was too much to comprehend, so she pushed aside all thoughts of it and focused on the conversation.

“Is everyone healthy?” Jessica almost hated to ask.

What if Cathy's family was sick? The fatality rate was ninety-five percent. If they were sick, they would most assuredly die.

"Yes," Cathy said, her voice sounding more confident. "It's been two days since Dean...well, since he passed. As soon as he started feeling sick, he locked himself in the bedroom and wouldn't come out." Her voice choked up. "Said he didn't want to expose us to the virus." It sounded like the tears were flowing freely. "I guess it worked because none of us got sick."

"He was a good man," Matt said.

Quiet sobs were the only reply.

"Do you..." Jessica began, then hesitated. "Do you know what's going on out there? I mean, the news reports have stopped and there doesn't seem to be any information on what's happening in our area."

"Didn't you get a flyer?" Cathy said, her emotions sounding more under control.

"A flyer?" Matt asked as he leaned closer to the phone. "What flyer?"

"Someone put flyers on all the doors earlier today about a meeting tomorrow afternoon. At the elementary school down the street."

"That sounds like a bad idea," Dylan said loud enough for all to hear. "If anyone's sick, they'll get the rest of the people sick."

CHAPTER 16

Matt

Matt agreed with Dylan. Putting healthy people in the same room as someone who was potentially sick sounded like a recipe for disaster.

"The flyer said not to come if you're sick," Cathy said.

Yeah, like everyone carrying the virus would know they were about to get sick. Matt shook his head.

"Are you going to the meeting?" Jessica asked.

"I don't know yet," Cathy said. "One of my boys doesn't want me to go but the other said we should. What about you? Are you going?"

"Unlikely," Matt said. "You probably should stay home too."

"I appreciate your concern, but I haven't decided yet."

Matt sighed. "Well, if you do go, will you tell us what you learn?"

"Yes."

"Thank you, Cathy," Jessica said. "Let's keep in touch. Okay?"

"That's a good idea. I don't...that is, I'm not sure how many people in our neighborhood are left."

After an uncomfortable silence, they said their good byes and disconnected.

"I'm going to see if there's a flyer on our door," Matt said as he stood. He put on a pair of gloves before going to the door.

"Be careful," Jessica said as she followed him.

Before opening the door, he looked out the front window to make sure no one was around, and when he felt confident that no one was, he unlocked the deadbolt, then opened the door a crack. A half-sheet of paper fluttered to the ground. He opened the door wider, then used his foot to drag the sheet inside before locking the door once again.

"The flyer," he said as he picked it up and held it like it was an important document heralding critical news.

"What's it say?" Jessica asked.

He held it so they both could read it. It said pretty much exactly what Cathy had told them. He pointed to the line that said *If you even suspect you may be sick, don't come.* "Can't be any more blunt than that."

One side of Jessica's mouth turned up in a wry smile. "They didn't even say please."

Matt was glad that whomever had created the flyer—and was presumably running the meeting—had been crystal clear. This person was no nonsense. A quality he admired.

"Should we go?" Jessica asked.

"I don't know. I'm leaning toward no. Besides, if Cathy goes, she can fill us in."

Jessica nodded. "True."

He was glad she agreed with him. The last thing he needed was to have an argument over something so risky.

"I'm going to see what I can find online," he said as he tossed the flyer and the gloves in the trash. The TV had only become good for entertainment. The only way to get news was on the Internet, which Matt had been scouring for information. Not a lot of official updates. The main source of information was social media, but the claims were so outlandish—*Whole cities were dead! This was a deliberate attack by a foreign country and they would drop a nuke next! #endoftheworld*—that Matt had a hard time believing much of what he read.

Still, he searched. He had to take advantage of access to the Internet while he could. He knew access wouldn't last. It couldn't. It was inevitable that the electricity would go off. With so many sick or dead, who was left to manage the power stations? So, after he tired of reading dubious reports posted by hysterical people, he spent the rest of his time printing off pages and pages of information about foraging for food, gardening, surviving off the land and anything else he could think of.

And then it happened.

The next morning the power went off. Moments later, Jessica burst into his office where he'd been in the middle of putting his latest print-outs into a binder that was nearly bursting at the seams.

"The power's off," she said, her eyes wide like she knew this was the end of civilization.

"I know." He didn't say this with sarcasm. Instead, he felt a deep sense of anxiety that took him by surprise. He'd been expecting this, yet it still shook him.

"Do you think it will come back on?"

"I don't know, but I wouldn't count on it."

The kids—all three of them plus Cleo—joined him and Jessica in his office.

"I guess you noticed the power's off," Kayla said, her forehead creasing.

Matt nodded, his gaze going to each of the kids, pausing on Brooke. She seemed to be adjusting reasonably well to being in their home. It also helped that she had Cleo with her. Matt had no idea what to do to make her feel at home besides treating her like one of the family. To him, she *was* part of the family now and he was happy to have her. So far she was pitching in without being asked and was generally pleasant to have around. Plus, having her there seemed to be keeping Dylan and Kayla from arguing like they sometimes did.

"Yeah," he finally said in reply. "We noticed."

"What's going to happen now?" Dylan asked, his brow wrinkling.

"Now," he said as he stood and faced the group, "we check the RV to make sure the power's working in there."

"You have power in your RV?" Brooke asked.

"Yeah," Dylan said, clearly proud that they had a solution.

"How?" she asked, her gaze shifting to Matt.

"There's a solar panel on the roof that powers the battery, and then there's an inverter that changes the battery power into 120 volt power which is the same thing we have in the house. As long as the sun is shining, we'll have power. Although it's not like the house. We have to conserve."

"So, at night there won't be any power?" Brooke asked.

"If we're careful with our usage during the day, the batteries will have enough juice to let us use the lights and charge our phones, but that's about it."

Kayla's eyes lit up. "We can still use our phones?"

Matt looked at her. "Yes, but I don't know how much longer cell service will be available. The carriers may no longer be up and running."

Her face fell. "Oh."

He thought about a bigger concern and couldn't hold back a grimace.

"What's wrong?" Jessica asked.

He didn't want to panic them, but they needed to know the score. "I'm concerned about how long water will flow."

All four pairs of eyes widened in response.

"That's why I filled the fresh water tank in the RV. Plus, I bought a lot of bottled water when I stocked up a Costco."

Jessica's forehead furrowed. "I wonder what everyone else is doing about the power going out? And, you know, just in general." She frowned. "I feel so isolated here. We have no idea what's going on in our own neighborhood."

Matt stared at her. "Are you suggesting we go to the meeting?"

She shrugged. "I'm not sure. I mean, how else are we going to find anything out now that the power's out? What if help is coming? Or, what if there's a vaccine. Or..." She shook her head. "If there's any news at all, we won't know. I mean, we can't rely on Cathy. We don't even know if she's going."

He hated the idea of risking his family's health, but Jessica had a point. Sighing heavily, he nodded. "Okay. I'll go. Alone."

"Uh-uh." Jessica shook her head. "You're not going alone. If you go, I go."

He looked at her implacable face and knew there would be no talking her out of it. "Fine."

With a grim smile, she nodded.

CHAPTER 17

Jessica

As Matt pulled into a parking space, Jessica found herself gripping the armrest, her nerves stretched tight. It felt strange to be out of the house after not leaving for a week. Who would be at the meeting? Were so many people dead that there would be very few attendees? But when she looked at the cars parked in the lot, she was surprised to see more than she'd expected.

"Masks on," Matt said before putting an earloop mask over his nose and mouth.

Jessica felt slightly foolish coming to this meeting wearing gloves and a face mask. The last time she'd been in public was before the bird flu had taken hold. But life had shifted at a crazy angle since then. This was the new normal and she doubted they'd be the only ones taking precautions.

She put her mask on and turned to Matt. "Ready." Her voice was slightly muffled.

Side by side, they walked toward the entrance to the school, but when they reached the main doors, they saw a sign stating that the meeting had been moved from the auditorium to the playground.

"Makes sense," Matt said through his mask. "With no power, it would be pitch black in the auditorium."

They turned and headed to the playground, which was around the back of the school.

"It'll be better to be outside," he added as they rounded the corner of the school. "We can keep more distance between us and whoever else is there."

"Good point."

As they approached the playground, they saw people talking in small groups, many of them also wearing face masks. A few wore bandanas over their mouths and noses. Mildly surprised to see that, Jessica turned to Matt with a sardonic smile. Then she realized he couldn't see her mouth. Frowning now, she said, "I guess a lot people had the same idea we had." Somehow that made her feel better. Like the others were just as concerned as she and Matt were with staying healthy.

"Or they're sick and don't want anyone to know," he murmured.

Alarmed at that idea, she slowed her pace.

Matt urged her forward. "We'll keep our distance from the others."

She nodded and they moved on, stopping a good ten feet away from everyone else.

A man was huddled with two other people at the edge of

the playground. He broke away and loudly said, "Can everyone hear me?"

Everyone turned toward him, nodding. Jessica nodded too. She could hear him fine. There were no children at the meeting either, and once the man had spoken, everyone fell silent. She looked him over, trying to decide if she'd seen him before. He looked like he was in his forties. Wearing jeans and a t-shirt, he was average height, wore glasses, had a nice head of hair, and seemed confident in front of the group. And he wasn't wearing any kind of covering on his face.

"Good," he said. "My name is Tony Webb. I head up the Neighborhood Watch program on my street." He chuckled. "That doesn't really mean anything, but I thought it might be helpful for us to get together as a neighborhood to discuss what we know and how we can help each other." His face became serious. "A lot of us have lost loved ones. I've, uh, I lost my wife and both my children." His chin quivered before he drew in a deep breath. "I buried all three of them myself." He was quiet a moment, then he sighed deeply. Finally, his gaze swept the assembled crowd. "I'm glad to see so many here. I, uh, I'd wondered if anyone would come."

Jessica thought about the man's courage in organizing this when he'd lost so much.

"To start, let's discuss what we know." With a grimace he said, "First, we know this flu is swift and deadly. Second, we know that the power has been off all day." One side of his mouth quirked up. "That's pretty much all I know." He looked at the group with expectation. "Does anyone else have any information?"

One man held up his hand.

Tony pointed to him. "Your name?"

"Bryant. Bryant Johnson."

"Okay, Bryant. What information do you have?"

Bryant cleared his throat. "I'm a Ham radio operator and I've been spending a lot of time on there lately."

That got everyone's attention.

"Do you know what's going on in other places?" Tony asked.

Jessica perked up. The news had been off the air for a few days, so she was intensely interested in what Bryant was going to say.

She felt someone touch her arm. Startled, she turned to see Cathy standing there. Despite the fact that it might offend her neighbor, Jessica backed up a few steps. Matt did as well. Cathy didn't have a mask and she'd had people in her family who'd had the virus. Jessica wasn't about to take any chances.

"Sorry," Cathy said, obviously understanding why Jessica had backed away. She glanced toward Tony. "Have I missed anything?"

Jessica shook her head, then gestured toward Bryant. "He was about to tell us what he's heard on his Ham radio."

Cathy nodded, then looked toward Bryant.

"It's bad all over," Bryant said without preamble. "People are dying from the bird flu in droves, stores are completely out of food which is leading to riots and mass chaos. The power's out in most cities." He paused. "Things are really ugly."

Jessica felt so isolated from all that. Besides their scary run-in with Jack several days earlier, they'd been safe and secure in their house.

"What about around here?" someone asked, directing the question to Bryant.

Bryant turned to the man who'd asked. "A lot of people didn't have more than a few days' worth of food, which has now run out." Bryant looked at the group. "People are getting desperate." He frowned deeply. "Desperate people do desperate things."

Quiet murmurs filled the air as a sense of panic began to take over.

"Let's not freak out yet," Tony said, settling the group down for the moment. "Let's focus on our group, our neighborhood." His lips compressed. "How are all of you set for food and water?"

Jessica looked at Matt. She would leave it to him to decide how much information to share with these people.

CHAPTER 18

Matt

Matt didn't know these people. They were neighbors, yes, but he didn't know them personally and wasn't ready to tell them that his family was well stocked up on food. Besides, he knew that many people in this area had been counseled by their church leaders to store a year's supply of food. He didn't know how many had done it, but he figured his neighborhood was better prepared than many others would be.

He waited to see if anyone would share the information Tony had asked for.

"We have sufficient for our needs," one man volunteered. "For now."

Matt saw others nodding in agreement. Good. If people were self-sufficient, that would benefit them all. Maybe he could even trade his surplus for things he didn't have.

"Is there anyone in need?" Tony asked as his gaze swept the assembled group.

A young couple raised their hands. "We're, uh," the man began, "that is to say, we've only been married a few months and money's been tight, so we haven't managed to be as prepared as we would have liked."

Tony nodded, then looked around the crowd. "Would anyone be willing to donate a few things to this couple?"

No one said anything.

"Okay. How about this?" Tony looked at the couple. "Tell us where you live and if anyone is so inclined, they can leave whatever they can spare on your porch."

The young husband stated his address, then added. "I can trade. I'm good at fixing things."

Tony nodded. "Excellent idea." Then he turned to the group. "Anyone else in need?"

A few other people raised their hands.

Matt quietly shook his head. He had mixed feelings. On the one hand, if people had spent more time and money preparing for an emergency rather than wasting it on fancy cars and toys, maybe they wouldn't be in need now. Then again, if Jessica hadn't called him that day and if he hadn't stocked up at Costco, they'd be living off their freeze-dried meals by now. So he couldn't exactly judge anyone else.

Tony held out his hand to someone nearby and that person handed him a clipboard. "If you're in need," he said, holding up the clipboard, "write down your address and the skills you have and I'm sure trades can be made."

As several people approached to write their information

down, Tony faced everyone else. "Do any of you have medical knowledge?"

One woman raised her hand.

"What about you?" Matt whispered to Jessica.

She shook her head. "I don't think a dental hygienist counts."

If she didn't want to say anything, he wouldn't push her. "Okay."

"What are your qualifications?" Tony asked the woman.

"I'm a physician. Dr. Maddie Larsen."

"Wonderful," Tony said as he jotted that down.

Matt agreed. Having someone in the neighborhood who could treat injuries or illnesses would be invaluable.

"Anyone in law enforcement?"

No one raised their hands.

"What about military experience?" Tony asked.

Three men raised their hands. All appeared to be in their early thirties.

"Excellent," he said with approval as he wrote down their names. "What other skills does everyone have?"

"I can fix pretty much anything," an older man offered.

"I'm a mechanical engineer," another man said.

Two men announced that they were electricians. Everyone joked that that skill may or may not be useful now.

"My husband's really handy," one woman stated, smiling at the tall man standing beside her.

Tony nodded approvingly. "I have to say, with just this relatively small group we have a decent number of critical skills covered." His gaze swept the small crowd. "Any hunters?"

No one raised their hands.

Tony frowned, then asked, "Any woodworkers?"

Jessica nudged Matt. He turned to her with a frown, then realized she couldn't see his mouth. Finally, he raised his hand. All eyes swiveled in his direction.

"Great! What's your name?"

"Matt. Matt Bronson."

As Tony wrote that down he asked, "What kind of woodworking do you do, Matt?"

Conscious that everyone was watching him and waiting for his reply, he cleared his throat. "Mostly furniture."

"Beautiful furniture," Jessica added loudly enough for all to hear.

Despite himself, pride welled up inside him. The pieces he'd built—dressers, bookshelves, tables—were custom and extremely nice.

Tony smiled. "So, you know how to use tools."

"Yeah, but without power, most won't work."

"True, but knowledge is what I'm after." Then he turned to the group. "Anyone with mechanical skills. Like, the ability to fix motors, cars, that kind of thing."

One man raised his hand.

After writing the man's name down, and with a wide smile, Tony said, "I wasn't sure how this meeting would go, but after hearing all that you have to say, I propose that we work together as a neighborhood to provide security and food for our small neck of the woods."

Heads nodded all around and excitement welled up inside Matt. Before this pandemic he'd never known his neighbors had so many skills. If he'd ever needed to hire someone to work on his house or car, he'd searched online to find people. Yet all along people with those skills had been right here. And to think that they could pool their skillsets now to create a little community right here. It was an awesome feeling.

"I'm glad we came to this meeting," Jessica said beside him.

He smiled at her, and though his mouth was covered, he knew his eyes reflected his feelings, and by the small crinkles around Jessica's eyes, she was just as excited about this as he was.

"If you all agree," Tony said, "I'd like to meet again in a few days so we can talk about challenges we're facing. I'd love it if, together, we can come up with ideas on how to better organize our group." When everyone nodded in agreement, he smiled. "We'll get flyers out again when we know exactly when we're meeting." He paused like he was considering his next words. "I don't want to put anyone in danger, but if you're willing, maybe you can check on your neighbors who aren't here and see if, well, see how they're doing."

Matt glanced at Jessica. She looked at him, her forehead creased.

"Okay," Tony said, "see you next time we meet."

"What if we need help between now and then?" someone called out.

"What is your name, sir?" Tony asked the man.

"Kevin."

With a nod, Tony turned to the crowd. "Any ideas on how to answer Kevin's question?"

Matt hadn't known what he'd expected out of this meeting, but he liked Tony. He was no-nonsense, yet not a dictator in any sense of the word. He liked how Tony didn't purport to have all the answers.

"Anyone?" Tony prompted with a smile that said he hoped *someone* had ideas.

To Matt's surprise, he raised his hand.

"Matt," Tony said with a smile that broadcast a bit of relief that someone had spoken up.

"What kind of help are you thinking of?" Matt asked Kevin.

"Security, mainly. I mean, now that things are rapidly falling apart, I'm concerned about outsiders coming to our neighborhood and causing trouble."

The thought had crossed Matt's mind too. Then, thinking of Jack, he almost wanted to add *There could also be trouble from neighbors*. Instead, Matt glanced at each of the men who'd said they had military experience. "What would you suggest?"

The men looked at each other, then one of them said, "If your family's threatened and you have a weapon, I suggest you use it."

Some people nodded, others looked kind of horrified. Whether it was because they thought they might have to shoot someone or because they couldn't believe society had come to this, he didn't know.

"Your name, sir?" Tony asked the man.

"Derrick." His voice was slightly muffled as he had a bandana covering his mouth and nose like some kind of outlaw.

"Can't we just call the police?" one woman asked.

"Have you tried calling 911 lately?" Jessica loudly asked.

The woman looked at Jessica, then shook her head.

"All you'll get is a busy signal," Jessica said.

"That's if your phone even works," Derrick said. "Without power, you won't be able to charge your cell phone. And even if you could, service will most likely be unavailable. Or will be unavailable soon."

As loud conversation filled the air, Matt was doubly glad he'd bought the 9mm and the rifle, and was especially glad he'd stocked up on ammo.

"I don't own a gun," one man said.

Matt looked at Derrick, who shook his head. "Don't know what to tell you, sir."

"Maybe we can put together patrols," Matt said. He didn't know why he was speaking up. He was a software engineer, not a security expert. Then again, maybe it was because of his run-in with Jack. He didn't want to have to be on his own protecting his family. Safety in numbers and all of that.

"Good idea, Matt," Tony said, then he turned to the

crowd. "Whoever's willing to be on patrol, please see Matt."

Matt's eyes widened. Just because he'd suggested the patrols didn't mean he wanted to be in charge. Before he had a chance to object, most of the men and a few women turned and walked toward him. To his relief, the three military men were also approaching.

He looked at Jessica. Was she surprised because he would be in charge or because so many people were headed their way?

CHAPTER 19

Matt

Things were moving fast. They'd come to the meeting to observe and suddenly Matt was responsible for security in their entire neighborhood? How had that happened?

Glad they were wearing gloves and face masks, when he saw Tony walking toward them with his clipboard in hand, he couldn't hold back a smile. It felt good to be part of this group where everyone wanted to help.

"Here you go," Tony said as he passed the clipboard to Matt, then he grinned. "In case you want to write anything down."

"You don't actually think I should be in charge of security, do you?" Matt asked with a wry smile as he took the clipboard and pen. Then he remembered he was wearing his mask so Tony wouldn't be able to see most of his facial expression.

Tony grinned. "That's totally up to you."

With a soft chuckle, Matt looked at the men and women approaching, his focus on the three guys who had military experience. "Which one of you wants to head up security?" he asked the three.

Derrick glanced at the other two men, none of whom volunteered, then said, "I will."

More than happy to hand it off, Matt held out the clipboard and pen. Derrick waved it off.

Feeling foolish for thinking Derrick would need it, Matt handed it back to Tony.

"First," Derrick said, looking at all of the people gathered around, "we need to monitor all major roads leading into our neighborhood. We need to control who has access. Second, we need to patrol in pairs, day and night, to keep an eye on what's happening." When everyone nodded in agreement, he gave a few pointers on what to look for when on patrol and added, "You'll need to supply your own weapons."

As he listened, Matt felt a sense of community. He didn't have to rely solely on himself. Others had expertise they were willing to share that would benefit all.

"What if I don't own a gun?" a man asked.

Derrick shifted his gaze to the man. "Do you know how to use one?"

The man shook his head.

Matt thought Derrick was frowning, but it was hard to tell since Derrick wore a bandana. "Anyone else need weapons training?"

Several hands went up.

"All right," Derrick said. "Meet here tomorrow morning at seven am sharp and I'll provide training."

"I'd like my teenagers to come," Matt said.

Derrick looked his way and nodded. "That's a good idea. The more people who know how to handle a weapon, the better."

Matt could feel Jessica fidgeting beside him and knew she couldn't be thrilled with his idea, but he agreed with Derrick. And if their family was threatened and he was incapacitated in any way, he didn't want his family to be helpless.

"Who's ready to begin patrolling tonight?" Derrick asked.

Matt, along with several others, raised his hand.

Derrick nodded at Matt. "You and I will take the midnight to four am shift." Then he assigned the other two military men with volunteers to take the earlier and later shifts.

Though Matt wasn't excited to have to be up in the middle of the night, he was pleased to be paired with Derrick. He had a feeling the man could teach him a lot.

The meeting broke up a short time later. Matt took a look at the clipboard before they left. As they drove home, he was more than glad they'd come.

"I'm going to the weapons training tomorrow," Jessica said after she pulled off her face mask.

Her statement took him by surprise but he was pleased

about it. Turning to her, he removed his mask as well. "Let's make it a family activity then."

She smirked. "A little different from game night, but yeah, I think that's a great idea."

"It'll be interesting to go on patrol with Derrick."

"He seems to know what he's doing."

Matt wholeheartedly agreed.

"I have to admit," she added with a frown. "I'm a little nervous about being home with just the kids while you're gone." Her frown deepened. "Especially with the power out."

He didn't like the idea of leaving his family either, but then he had an idea. "Tell you what. Let's use the power in the RV to charge up our walkie talkies. That way you can contact me if you need me." He turned to her with a smile. "We'll just be in our neighborhood, so we should stay in range."

With a look of relief, she said, "Great idea."

They pulled into their driveway. The second they entered the house, the kids peppered them with questions.

"How many people were there?"

"Was anyone sick?"

"What'd you guys talk about?"

Matt held up one hand. "Family meeting."

At that, the five of them went into the family room and sat down. The kids looked nervous, like Matt was about to deliver bad news. To counteract that, he smiled. "Tomorrow morning at seven you're all going to weapons training."

"Yes!" Dylan shouted with a fist pump, but both Kayla and Brooke seemed less enthusiastic.

"What for?" Kayla asked.

"I don't like guns," Brooke said.

"I'm going too," Jessica said with a soft smile.

The girls looked at her, their mouths falling open.

"Really?" Kayla asked.

"Why?" Brooke said.

"All right, Mom," Dylan said with a wide grin.

Time to take control of the conversation. "All of us need to be comfortable with how to use a gun," Matt said. "The way things are heading…" He let his sentence trail off. He didn't want to scare them. Especially Brooke. She'd been through more than anyone should ever have to go through. But they needed to know the truth, needed to be prepared. "To keep us safe, we all need to know how to use a weapon safely."

Dylan's smile grew, if that was possible, but the girls looked even less certain.

"I've never touched a gun before," Brooke admitted.

Kayla looked at her friend. "Neither have I, but I guess…" She glanced at Matt before turning back to Brooke. "I guess it would be a good idea to, you know, not be scared of them."

Glad she was getting on board, Matt smiled. "You'll be trained by a military vet. Derrick."

"Derrick Weathers?" Brooke asked.

"Yeah. I think that was his last name."

Brooke seemed to relax. "I know him. He lives two

houses down and across the street from me." Her face fell. "Well, from where I used to live."

"It's still your house, Brooke," Matt quietly said.

Her gaze went to her lap, but she nodded.

Wanting to take away the melancholy she was feeling, Matt said, "So, you know Derrick?"

She lifted her eyes and met his gaze. "Yeah. He helped my dad lay sod last year. He seemed like a nice guy."

"I'll be going on patrol with him tonight."

"Patrol?" Dylan said, smiling with enthusiasm. "Cool." Then he looked at Matt with undisguised hope. "Can I come?"

"It's not up to me. Derrick's in charge of security. But I suspect he'll want you to get that training before he'll let you come on patrol."

"He's too young to patrol," Jessica said beside him, her tone urgent.

"Carl was taking out bad guys when he was, like, twelve."

"Carl?" Jessica asked.

"Yeah," Dylan said. "On The Walking Dead."

Matt forced down a chuckle.

"That's just a TV show," Jessica pointed out.

"Maybe," Dylan said in reply, "but the world fell apart on that show and it's falling apart now."

True as that was, Matt didn't want Dylan to think this was all fun and games. "This is real life, Dylan. Not a TV show. We can't script how things go. Even good guys are going to get hurt."

Jessica jabbed Matt in the side. He looked at her and saw her glancing meaningfully at Kayla and Brooke. Both looked extremely worried.

"That's why we're going to have patrols," he said, hoping to assuage their fears. "To keep the bad guys away and keep our neighborhood safe."

"Which reminds me," Jessica said, standing. "Let's charge up those walkie talkies."

"Uh, Mom," Dylan said with a tone that said *duh*, "the power's off."

Matt stood and tapped Dylan on the back. "That's why we're going to use the RV's power."

His face brightened. "Oh. Right."

With that, the five of them plus Cleo trooped out to the RV.

CHAPTER 20

Jessica

Once Matt unlocked the door to the RV and held the door for her, Jessica stepped inside and pressed the buttons to open the three slide-outs. The space became much larger. Even so, Jessica tried to imagine what it would be like if they had to live in the small space—all five of them plus a dog. There was a small bedroom with a queen size bed for her and Matt, and in the corner of the main space was a bunk bed with a double mattress on the bottom and a twin on top. There was also a small table, a couch that converted into a bed, and a tiny kitchen. They'd been on dozens of camping trips in this RV, and they'd loved every trip, but it had always been nice to get home where they could spread out. With no power in the house, come winter it was possible they'd need to sleep in the RV. Assuming they had enough propane. If they managed to keep their propane tanks filled, they'd be able to stay warm.

Cleo made herself at home, stretching out on the laminate wood floor in front of the couch.

"Where are the walkie talkies?" Matt asked as he pulled open cabinets.

"Right here," Jessica said as she opened a drawer and took the walkies out along with the charging base. She set everything on the counter, and after Matt pressed the button to turn on the inverter, she plugged the base in. A tiny light glowed red, indicating that the charging base had power.

Glad that they'd sprung for the solar panels and inverter when they'd bought the RV several years earlier, Jessica wondered what everyone in their neighborhood would do if they needed electricity for critical items. Then she wondered what would happen if everyone discovered that they had access to power. The thought sent a zing of panic up her spine.

"Hey, guys," she said, her voice tense.

"What's up?" Matt asked.

"I think it would be best if we kept this," she swept her hand toward the charging walkie talkies, "a secret."

"The walkie talkies?" Kayla asked, her nose wrinkled in confusion.

"The electricity," Matt said. "I agree. This is information we need to keep on the down-low."

"Okay," Brooke said.

"How come?" Kayla asked at the same time.

"If everyone knows," Dylan said, "then everyone will want to use it."

"Is that a bad thing?" Kayla asked.

Jessica looked to Matt. He said, "If people find out, we'll have a line a mile long. It would tax the system. Besides, it would probably be for useless things like cell phones."

"Useless?" Kayla asked, her eyes wide. "Why would a cell phone be useless?"

"Do you have service?" Jessica asked as she sat on the small couch. The last time she'd checked her phone was before the power had gone out so she didn't know if service was even available.

"Yeah," Kayla said.

"Really?" Matt asked as he took his phone from his pocket. He looked at his screen, tapped on an icon, then said, "I don't."

Kayla grinned. "Well, I do." Then, to prove it, she took her phone out of her pocket and looked at the screen. "Wait." She tapped a few icons as panic swept over her face. "I did before."

"I'm sorry, sweetie," Jessica said. "With the power out in so many places it was inevitable that service would go out too."

"That sucks," Kayla said, her face glum as she shoved her phone into her back pocket.

"When power comes back on," Brooke said with hope in her eyes, "cell service will be back, right?"

Jessica thought about the report Bryant had given—that

power was out all across the country—and decided her children shouldn't have false hope. "*If* it comes back on."

"What do you mean?" Kayla asked. "It always comes back on."

"It's different this time," Matt said.

"Wait," Dylan said like reality was just starting to sink in, "it's not coming back on? Like, no more TV? No more video games?"

Jessica wouldn't miss TV or video games. Other things—critical things—would be much harder to go without. No more lights, no more washing machine, no more refrigerator, no more oven or microwave.

"That's right," Matt said, cutting into her thoughts. "Too many people have..." his eyes slid to Brooke before going back to Dylan, "died. No more people to fix or maintain the electrical grid."

The kids began listing all the things they would miss, and when Jessica realized that nearly every single thing she did relied on electricity, a sense of dread began sweeping over her.

"Okay," she said abruptly, cutting off Dylan's long lament over how hard it was going to be without video games. Everyone looked at her. "Enough whining because you're not even going to care about electricity if you have no food."

Kayla's eyes widened. "We have food. Dad bought a lot."

A pinched look came over Dylan. "We'll have to scavenge."

Jessica hadn't meant to spark panic, but her children were focusing on the wrong things.

"We won't have to scavenge for a while," Matt said. "We should be set for now, but we have to be careful."

"Wait," Kayla said as she held up both hands, "are you saying we'll *eventually* have to scavenge?" She looked horrified by the idea.

"It'll be cool," Dylan said. "We can go into people's houses." One side of his mouth quirked up. "I mean the houses where everyone's dead. And we can take whatever we want."

This conversation was all kinds of wrong. Jessica had to put a stop to it. "Enough." She audibly sighed. "Let's go back in the house. We need to better organize our food and update our inventory list." She looked at Matt. "We need to keep better track of what we have."

"Good idea."

Brooke held up her hand with a grimace.

"What's wrong, Brooke?" Jessica asked with a soft smile.

"Speaking of food. I, uh, I'm just about out of dog food for Cleo."

"Oh."

"Do you have more at your house?" Matt asked.

She nodded. "We have a lot. Dad..." Her eyes filled with tears. They gave her the time she needed to get her emotions under control. "He'd just gone to the store before...well, before."

Jessica's eyes shifted to Matt. He looked back at her and

she knew he was thinking the same thing she was. That they could add the food from Brooke's house to their supplies.

Matt looked at Brooke. "We can go to your house and get Cleo's dog food." He paused. "Would it be okay with you if we brought the food from your house here?"

Brooke smiled. "Of course. I've, uh, I've been thinking we should do that but I didn't know if you'd want to."

Relieved she was okay with them basically raiding her house, Jessica went to Brooke's side and wrapped an arm around her shoulder, then she looked at Matt. "When do you want to go."

His gaze went to each person. "Right away."

They stepped out the RV. Matt brought up the rear, locking the door behind him.

CHAPTER 21

Matt

"Are you sure you want to come?" Matt asked Brooke as they prepared to take a trip to her house.

She nodded. "When Dad…," she blinked several times, "when he died, I…I buried him in the backyard." She dragged in a deep breath. "And Mom…well, she died at the hospital."

Amazed at her strength, Matt didn't know what to say.

"I didn't know about…," Kayla said beside her, "well, about what you did with your dad."

Nodding, Brooke smiled sadly at Kayla.

"We'd better get going," Matt said. It was getting late and he wanted to get this taken care of right away. He kissed Jessica. "Will you be okay here by yourself?"

They'd decided one person should stay behind to keep an eye on things.

Jessica nodded. "Yes. Besides, Cleo will be with me."

That actually did make Matt feel better. He turned to the kids. "All right. Let's go." He led the way to the front door and out to his truck.

When they pulled up to Brooke's house, Matt wasn't sure what he'd expected to find, but all was calm. No one was around. They got out and walked to the front door together.

"I have the key," Brooke said. She inserted the key and disengaged the lock, then twisted the doorknob. The door swung inward.

Matt waited. It was Brooke's house. She should go in first.

After a moment's hesitation, she stepped inside, then turned to them. "Come in."

They followed her in.

"Where do you keep the dog food?" Matt asked. He wanted to get what they needed and get out.

"In the pantry," she said before leading the way.

When Matt saw all the food they had in their pantry, he was more glad than ever that he'd asked if they could gather her food to bring back to their house.

"Do you have any boxes we can use?" he asked Brooke.

She looked like she was working hard to hold her emotions together. "Yeah. We have some plastic buckets in the basement."

Out of habit, Matt flipped the light switch at the top of the stairs to the basement. Nothing happened.

"I've got it, Dad," Dylan said, then he turned on a flashlight.

It was going to be hard to get used to no electricity.

Brooke led the way, showing them where the plastic buckets where as well as the small amount of food they had stored down there. A few cans of flour and rice sat on the shelves. Matt eyes widened in pleased surprise. He'd been worried about having an extra mouth to feed, but Brooke's contribution would certainly go a long way to mitigate his concern.

With Brooke's permission, Matt looked around the house for other supplies they could use. He gathered blankets, vitamins and other medications, as well as some hand tools Brooke's father kept in the garage.

With everyone's help, it took twenty minutes to load all of the supplies into his truck. Brooke took some time to gather her most precious personal belongings, and then they drove back to their house. Matt backed into the garage and everyone pitched in, carrying all the goods into the house.

"Wow," Jessica said with a smile as he set a large plastic bucket filled with food on the kitchen counter. "This will really help."

"I was thinking," Matt said as he surveyed their bounty before looking at each member of the family. "We have so much and so many others are in need. What if, I don't know, we brought some to those who need it?"

Jessica smiled. "I think that's a great idea." She looked thoughtful. "Maybe that young couple from the meeting."

He grinned. "I was thinking the same thing. I saw their address on the clipboard."

"What if we doorbell ditch them?" Kayla said. "Like, put it on their porch, then run away?"

Dylan's hand shot up. "I'm the fastest. I should do it."

They all laughed.

"Okay," Matt said. "We'll sneak over there right before dark."

"Shouldn't we go after dark?" Dylan asked.

Matt shook his head. "I don't want to scare them by knocking on their door too late at night."

"Aw," Dylan said, his face serious. "Makes sense."

Brooke nodded. "This is going to be awesome."

As the sun was beginning to set, Matt and his family got in his truck. Each of the three kids held a small bag with a variety of canned and other non-perishable goods. In the end, they'd decided to drop off food to the homes of three families—the young couple, and two families they knew had small children who'd raised their hands that they were in need. In all reality, it wouldn't go far, but the idea of doing what he could for his community felt right to Matt.

It didn't take long to drop the food on the porch, knock on the door, then dash away, and by the time they got home, they were all feeling much better about life in general.

CHAPTER 22

Matt

Just before midnight, Matt set a charged walkie talkie by Jessica's side of the bed, then leaned over and gave her a lingering kiss. "If you need anything, let me know."

"Do you have to go?" She sat up and looked at him, her forehead furrowed.

Though some moonlight trickled in through the open blinds, it was still quite dark. Without street lamps to cast light into their room, it felt eerie. He knew she was nervous about being left on her own, but he'd committed to patrol with Derrick for the next four hours.

"I'm sorry," he said as he sat on the edge of the bed. "Derrick's counting on me."

Softly sighing, she glanced at the walkie, then met his gaze. "I know."

"Try to go back to sleep."

She chuckled at that. "Fat chance."

He reached out and gently stroked her cheek. "I won't be far. Just around the neighborhood."

She nodded, then pulled him in for another kiss.

"You're making it hard to leave," he murmured against her lips.

Quietly laughing, she said, "Good."

He drew away before standing. "My shift is done at four."

She nodded. "Be safe, Matt. I love you."

"I love you too."

He turned and left the room, then went downstairs to gather what he needed, including a loaded .45 with an extra magazine. As he put the pistol in his inside-the-waistband belt holster, he felt strange. As a Concealed Carry Permit holder, he'd bought the holster long ago, but he hadn't really used it all that much. Now though, knowing he may need his weapon to protect his neighborhood, putting his pistol in the holster felt like a whole new level of responsibility.

Holding back a sigh, he shrugged into his jacket before putting the extra magazine into one of the pockets and the walkie talkie into the other. Then, after affixing the earloop mask over his mouth and nose, he headed out the door, locking the deadbolt behind him.

Walking toward the rendezvous point—the corner of a nearby street—he couldn't help but notice how abnormally quiet it was. No hum of a streetlamp or other mechanical things, no cars driving by, no porch lights to emit light across yards. A lone dog barked as Matt walked past a pitch black house. How many pets had died from starvation because their owners had died of the virus? The thought made him inexorably sad. He was glad they'd taken Cleo in. She would be an asset to their home—an extra level of defense.

"Don't move," a deep voice said next to his ear as something hard pressed against his neck. Was it a gun? Was he about to be shot?

Frozen in place, Matt thought he was going to wet himself. Volunteering to come out in the middle of the night, alone, during the early days of the apocalypse? What had he been thinking? He was no hero. He was just a man trying to protect his family.

Then it occurred to him. His family was alone. Who was this person and were others with him? Was his family in imminent danger? He had to get back to them, had to protect them.

Adrenaline dumped into his veins, and without thinking he spun away from his attacker. Ready to fight for his life, when Matt saw who was standing there, his mouth fell open.

"Derrick?" He wasn't wearing the bandana over his mouth and nose.

Derrick scowled and shook his head. "You need to gain situational awareness, Matt. If I'd been a bad guy, you'd be dead."

Was that why he'd done that? To wake Matt up? To scare him? Fury, powerful and swift, slammed into Matt and it took everything in him not to come at Derrick. Then again, he had the distinct feeling that Derrick could easily take him down. Instead, he glared at him. "Did you have a gun pressed to my neck?" Maybe the guy was mentally unstable.

Derrick smirked and held up his black-gloved hand, his middle and pointer fingers squeezed together. He'd only been pressing his fingers into Matt's neck. Not a gun.

Though still angry, Matt felt his fury drain away, replaced by embarrassment. He'd nearly wet himself over a finger pressed to his neck? "Not cool."

Derrick made a scoffing sound. "What's *not cool* is you walking along like you're still in your safe little neighborhood, not paying attention to anything around you. Anyone could have come up to you and…" He shook his head. "I'm not gonna go into all the ways you could have been compromised." One side of his mouth quirked up. "I think you got the idea."

As annoyed as Matt was, he couldn't fault Derrick for making a very convincing point. He reminded himself that when Derrick had told him they would partner on the patrol, Matt had been eager to learn from him. Well, that was certainly happening.

"Yeah," Matt said. "You made your point."

Derrick chuckled. "Good." He gestured with his head in the direction Matt had been walking. "We'll head up Rosewood Drive to start."

Evidently, Derrick had a plan, so Matt simply nodded and began walking beside him.

"Look, man," Derrick said with a sardonic laugh and talking in a quiet voice, "sorry if I scared the crap out of you."

Not wanting to admit that he'd almost peed himself, Matt forced a quiet laugh of his own. "I'll get over it."

Derrick nodded, but his attention was on the neighborhood. "You gotta keep your head on a swivel at all times."

"Right." All was silent in the neighborhood, not even the flicker of candlelight in any of the windows. Of course, it was after midnight so everyone was probably asleep. Matt's gaze swept across all of the houses within view, many with a red X on the door. "How many bodies do you think are in these houses?"

Derrick looked at him sharply as they walked, staring at him for several moments before going back to probing the neighborhood with his eyes. "Too many," he finally murmured.

"Do you think we ought to...I don't know...do something about them? The bodies, I mean." As Matt spoke, his eyes were in constant motion. No way was he going to let someone sneak up on him again.

"Like what?"

"Bury them? Burn them?"

Derrick snorted a laugh. "You can bring it up at the next neighborhood meeting. Maybe Tony will put a committee together."

"That's actually a good idea."

They reached a cross street. Derrick paused on the corner, slowly looking in each direction. Finally, they began crossing the street, but Derrick never stopped looking.

If this was how Derrick operated, and if he trained the others to be as vigilant, their neighborhood would be one of the safest places around.

Matt's walkie talkie squawked in his pocket, then Jessica, her voice urgent, said, "Matt! Matt, are you there?"

CHAPTER 23

Matt

Ignoring the look of surprise on Derrick's face, Matt yanked the walkie out of his pocket and pressed the button to reply. "I'm here. What's wrong?"

"I heard a noise outside and when I looked out the window I saw something moving. And Cleo's barking like crazy."

Matt could hear the barking. "Are the kids in the house?"

"Yes. They're right here with me."

Matt glanced at Derrick, who nodded once. "Okay. We'll be right there." Matt dropped the walkie into his pocket and spun around, taking off at a fast jog. They were about half a mile from his house.

Four minutes later they approached Matt's house. Matt was panting, but Derrick was breathing normally. Half annoyed, but also grateful to have him there, Matt stopped beside a thick tree trunk two houses away from his own, then bent over to catch his breath. "How do you want to do this?"

"First, turn off your walkie. You don't want to give your position away."

"Right." He pressed the button and whispered, "Jess, I'm here. Are you okay?"

"Yes."

"I'm going to turn my walkie off for now."

"Okay."

He shut it off, then stuffed in his jacket pocket.

Derrick gave him a long look. "If someone's in your yard, are you prepared to shoot? Knowing the person will most likely die?"

That gave him pause. Was he ready to be responsible for the death of another person? Then he pictured his family. Would he kill in order to protect them? Unequivocally, yes.

"If the person presents a threat," he said, "yes."

Derrick tilted his head. "How will you decide if the person presents a threat?"

Matt had no idea. "How do you decide that kind of thing?"

The sound of glass shattering filled the air. Both men jerked their heads in the direction of Matt's house.

"I think it came from the back of my house," Matt said as his heart slammed against his ribs.

Without another word, Derrick pulled a gun out of a holster and took off toward Matt's house. Matt took the .45 out of his holster and raced after him.

Moments later they stood outside the gate to Matt's backyard. Derrick held a finger to his lips, then he gave hand signals which Matt took to mean that Derrick would go through this gate while Matt should go through the gate on the other side of the house.

Nodding, and with his heart going a hundred miles an hour, Matt made his way across the front of his house, across the driveway, and to the gate on the other side. Drawing in a deep, lung-filling breath before slowly exhaling, he forced himself to calm down. Then he quietly, quietly, unlatched the gate before slowly pushing it inward.

On the look-out for an intruder, he peered around the edge of the gate, his gaze shooting in all directions

"On the ground!" he heard Derrick shout.

Alarmed that there actually was someone in his yard, Matt hustled through the side yard and around to the back to find a man on the ground with Derrick's knee in his back. The moon was hidden behind clouds so it was impossible to see who the man was.

Grateful that he hadn't had to deal with this on his own, Matt watched as Derrick expertly zip-tied the man's wrists behind his back.

"Who is it?" Matt asked.

Once the man was restrained, Derrick rolled him over and shone a flashlight into his face. The man squeezed his eyes closed against the bright light.

"I don't know his name," Derrick said, "but he was at the meeting today."

Now that he mentioned it, Matt remembered seeing the man at the back of the group of security volunteers.

"What's your name?" Matt asked as he squatted beside him.

Fear shone from the man's eyes. "Charlie. Charlie Swenson."

"What are you doing in my backyard, Charlie?" Matt felt a mixture of anger and confusion. He lifted his gaze to the now-broken window in his dining room, then he scowled at the man. "And why in the heck did you break my window?"

"I…I was desperate," Charlie began. "My family's starving and I…I needed food."

"What made you think I had any?"

"You…you didn't raise your hand to say you needed anything. So, I figured…" He did a half-shrug.

Still confused why he had been a target, Matt said, "So did a lot of people."

"I knew you'd be on patrol, so I thought I'd…" He let his words trail off.

Realizing that Charlie had *planned* to break into his home when he wasn't there and when his wife and children would be asleep and vulnerable, Matt felt an overwhelming rage descend over him. What if Jessica had caught him? Would he have hurt her? *Killed* her? And what about Kayla and Dylan and Brooke?

Without thinking, he pressed his gun to Charlie's temple. "I should shoot you right now." His teeth were clenched as he spoke.

"Matt," Derrick said beside him, breaking through his rage.

With his gun still buried in Charlie's forehead, Matt lifted his gaze to Derrick. Derrick glanced meaningfully at the gun, then raised his eyebrows.

Shocked to realize he'd been on the verge of killing a man in cold blood, Matt pulled the gun away from Charlie's head.

Charlie exhaled loudly, his breath ragged, his eyes on Derrick. "Thank you."

Making a scoffing sound, Derrick shook his head. "Don't thank me. I'm going to lock you up and let the neighborhood decide what to do with you."

"Is there anyone else with you?" Matt asked, his mind still racing and his heart still pounding.

"No," Charlie said. "It was just me."

Matt looked at Derrick. How could they be sure Charlie wasn't lying? What if someone else was waiting to make a play once Matt and Derrick left?

Derrick pressed a forearm across Charlie's throat. "You wouldn't lie to us, would you, Charlie?"

Charlie mouthed the word *No* and shook his head, at least as much as he could with Derrick's powerful forearm crushing his throat. Tears filled the man's eyes.

Derrick glanced at Matt, who nodded. He believed him.

Derrick lifted his arm and Charlie gasped for breath.

"I'm sorry," Charlie said, his voice strained. "I'll do whatever you guys decide. I know it was wrong. I was just..." His face crumpled. "My family hasn't eaten in days. They're...they're starving.

Though Matt felt sorry for him, he was also furious with the solution Charlie had chosen, which had put his family in danger. "You could've traded for food."

"I...I don't have any skills to trade."

Matt shook his head.

"Get up," Derrick said as he roughly pulled the man to his feet.

Matt wondered what they were supposed to do with him now. They couldn't call 911, not without cell service—not that anyone would answer. Besides, as far as he knew, the police were no more.

CHAPTER 24

Jessica

Stunned to see her husband pointing a gun at a man —no, he was doing more than pointing. He looked like he was going to shoot him—Jessica held her breath as she peered around the edges of the sliding glass door that led to the backyard.

"What's happening?" Dylan asked from behind her.

She'd made the children stay back and now she was glad. She didn't want them to see their father killing a man.

Then she saw Matt look at Derrick before taking the gun away from the man's head. Exhaling in relief, when she saw Derrick pull the man to his feet, she unlocked the door and slid it open before stepping onto the patio.

"Matt?" she said as her gaze went to the man whose hands were tied behind his back. "What's happening?"

Matt looked at her, his face a kaleidoscope of emotions.

"We've got it under control," Derrick said.

"Whoa," Dylan said from beside her.

"What's going on?" Kayla asked. "Is Dad okay?"

With a glance at her daughter, Jessica said, "He's fine."

Matt stepped toward her and she rushed forward, overwhelmed by all that had happened, was still happening. He drew her into his arms. Savoring the feeling of security his embrace sent over her, Jessica whispered, "What happened?"

Matt pulled away and looked at her with a frown before telling her about how the man, Charlie—someone from their own neighborhood!—had planned to break in and had gotten as far as breaking a window.

Shocked, Jessica looked at the man, vaguely recalling him from the earlier meeting. "What's going to happen now?"

Matt looked at Derrick, who said, "Your husband and I will take him somewhere where he can't cause trouble. In the morning the neighborhood will have to figure out what to do with him."

Jessica shifted her eyes to Matt. She spoke in a low voice so the kids couldn't hear. "You're leaving me alone? Now? What if..." She looked at Charlie. "What if someone else tries to do the same thing?"

Guilt and concern swept over Matt's face, but before he could speak, Dylan placed a hand on her arm. "I'll keep you safe, Mom."

"No," she said as she turned to him. "That's your father's job."

"He has to patrol."

"Dylan's right," Matt said, which annoyed Jessica. Yes, she cared about the neighborhood, but didn't Matt think his own family came first?

"Look," Derrick said to the group, "I'll grab someone else to take Matt's shift. Tonight."

Relieved, Jessica smiled at Derrick. "Thank you."

"I suggest you come to the weapons training tomorrow," he added, his gaze right on Jessica.

"I was already planning on it." Hating the feeling of being helpless and vulnerable, she was determined to learn how to protect herself.

Derrick grinned, his teeth gleaming white in the moonlight. "Awesome. See you in the morning." With his hand firmly gripping the man's arm, Derrick walked out of their yard and into the night.

Kayla pointed to the broken window. "Can we cover that up?"

Matt frowned. "I don't think I have enough plywood, but I'll check." With flashlight in hand, he went inside with Dylan right behind him.

Jessica led the girls inside and a few minutes later Matt was back with a small sheet of plywood.

"You had one?" Jessica asked, grateful her husband enjoyed woodworking, which is why he had random pieces of wood on hand.

"Yeah," he said, "but it'll only cover half of the broken window."

"Better than nothing," she said, although the idea of

anyone being able to climb through the glass without them knowing set her nerves on edge.

Matt must have thought the same thing, because he said, "I'll keep watch tonight and tomorrow we'll get more plywood."

Too tired to think about what they needed to do the next day, Jessica nodded, and after Matt and Dylan nailed the plywood over half of the broken window, she gave Matt a kiss, then led the kids upstairs where they all went to bed.

It took a while for her to settle back in for the night, especially without Matt by her side, but eventually she drifted off.

Early the next morning when the sun streamed through the window, she woke abruptly. She hadn't slept well—she'd been on high alert all night listening for any sounds that didn't belong. And with the power out, every little creak of the house woke her. But now, in the light of a new day, she felt better, less worried.

At breakfast, as the five of them sat around the table eating, Jessica turned to Matt. "Should one of us stay here and, I don't know, guard our supplies? I mean, after last night I'm worried that someone else will try to break in."

Matt, who looked exhausted after keeping watch most of the night, nodded. "I was thinking the same thing. You and the kids go to Derrick's training. I'll stay here and keep an eye on things."

Though Jessica would have preferred that Matt come with them, she knew his suggestion was the best one. She and the kids needed this training. How else to defend themselves and their home?

She placed her hand on his and smiled. "All right."

"Can you ask Derrick to stop by later?" Matt asked as she and the kids were walking out the door.

"Sure."

Wearing face masks, Jessica and the three kids walked the half mile to the school. When they arrived, Jessica saw a small group of people, many of them wearing something over their mouths and noses. Jessica wondered if the virus was still running rampant or if it was burning itself out.

"Everyone circle around," Derrick called out to the small crowd, his mouth and nose covered by a bandana. A number of different size guns were lying on a small table beside where he stood.

Once it looked like everyone had arrived, he began.

"Rule number one," he said as he lifted a gun from the table and pointed it at the ground, "always assume a gun is loaded."

Everyone listened with rapt attention as he discussed several other safety tips and then let each person who wanted to take a turn hold whichever gun they wanted.

When it was Dylan's turn, Jessica could see how excited he was to get his hands on a gun. Partly glad he wasn't afraid, but also wishing he was, at least a little, she watched as Derrick worked with Dylan one on one on how to check to see if a bullet was in the chamber, which it wasn't, and how to rack the slide.

"Can we practice shooting?" Dylan asked, his eyes alight with interest.

"Good question," Derrick said, then he faced the group. "The best way to become comfortable with firearms is to use one. I'll scout out a place where we can safely have target practice."

He pointed to a clipboard on the table. "If you're interested in target practice, write down your name and address and I'll make sure you're informed of where and when."

When the lesson was over, Jessica waited until everyone who wanted to talk to Derrick had left before she approached him.

"Where's Matt?" he asked as he loaded his guns into a bag.

"After what happened we decided it would be a good idea to, you know, guard our supplies."

Derrick frowned, then nodded. "Yeah. I can see why you'd want to do that."

She pictured the man who'd nearly broken into her house. "Where's Charlie?"

"In a secure location."

Jessica had no idea what that meant, but obviously Derrick didn't want to get into details, so she just nodded. "Matt wanted me to ask if you'd stop by our place."

He hefted his bag over his shoulder. "Sure thing."

CHAPTER 25

Matt

When a knock sounded at the front door an hour after Jessica and the kids had returned from their training with Derrick, Matt's heart hammered in his chest. Was it Derrick, or someone who would cause Matt and his family trouble?

He'd been dozing on the couch, but the confident knock had jerked him awake.

"I'll get it," he said to Jessica as he stood. She and the kids were in the kitchen stocking the pantry with food from the basement storage room. He and Jessica had been trying to figure out a way to secure their supplies so that they could leave the house without guarding it. So far they hadn't come up with a good idea.

With a slight sense of trepidation, Matt approached the front door. "Who is it?" he called out.

"Derrick."

Relieved, Matt unlocked the door and pulled it open. "Thanks for coming by."

"What's up?"

Matt invited him in and Derrick stepped inside. Neither of them were wearing coverings on their faces, but Matt felt confident that Derrick wasn't sick.

"I need to get some plywood for my broken window." Not sure how Derrick would respond to his idea, Matt hesitated. Then he glanced toward the kitchen—he hadn't told Jessica his idea either. "I was thinking you and I could make a trip to Home Depot." He spoke softly so Jessica wouldn't hear. No reason to get her upset until he was certain they were going.

Derrick glanced in the direction of the broken window.

"I had enough plywood to cover half of the window," Matt said, "but that's not going to work."

Derrick rubbed his jaw, then he exhaled before nodding. "Yeah. I'll go. I can pick up a few things myself."

Elated that he would have a strong ally with him, Matt grinned. "Sweet."

Derrick chuckled. "You might change your mind once we get there."

Matt tilted his head. "Why do you say that?"

"It just might be a bit different than the trips to Home Depot you're used to. I mean, I doubt they're actually up and running."

Truth be told, Matt had assumed the same thing, but it was hard to picture what it would actually be like. "Right."

"When do you want to go?"

"Now?"

"Okay." Derrick looked thoughtful. "We'll take my truck."

That was fine with Matt.

"We'll need to carry."

Matt knew he meant they would need to bring guns. He already had his .45 in his waist holster. After all the craziness with Jack and then Charlie, he wanted to be ready for anything. "You think we'll need to use them?" The thought was kind of nuts. He was running a quick errand, not going to war.

Derrick's shoulders lifted in a shrug. "Gotta be prepared for anything."

Matt nodded. "I just need to tell Jessica where I'm going." He knew his tone broadcast that this trip would be news to his wife.

"Okay. I'll be out front."

After Derrick left, Matt went into the kitchen. Jessica was on a step stool putting cans on the highest shelf.

"How's it going?" he asked.

"Good," she said as she turned around. "What did you want with Derrick?"

Here goes. "He's going to help me get some plywood."

Her face brightened. "Great! Does he have some we can use?"

"Not exactly."

Her eyes narrowed. "What aren't you telling me?"

The kids all stopped what they were doing to watch the exchange.

"Derrick and I are going to Home Depot."

"Oh."

"Can I go?" Dylan asked.

"No," he and Jessica both said at the same time.

Huffing out a loud sigh, Dylan turned back to taking cans of carrots out of a box and placing them on the counter.

Jessica came around the counter and walked into the family room, motioning for Matt to follow. "Is that safe?" She'd kept her voice low so the kids wouldn't hear.

He didn't want her to worry, but he wasn't going to lie. "I don't know, but that's why I wanted Derrick to come."

Her lips pursed. "Is there any other way?"

"Besides knocking on every door in the neighborhood to see who has plywood they'll hand over? No."

Her shoulders drooped like she knew going to Home Depot was the best option. Then she threw her arms around him. "Please be careful."

"I will," he murmured in her ear.

She stared at him a moment, then smiled. "Can you pick up packets of vegetable seeds?"

Matt chuckled. "Anything else?"

"Potting soil and seed starting trays."

"Will do." He gave her a kiss, then, after grabbing two face masks, two pairs of gloves, and two flashlights, he went out front and walked toward Derrick's truck.

It was an older truck, not fancy or expensive. In fact, Matt could see a spot of rust here and there. There was a hard shell over the bed of the truck. He just hoped the engine was in decent shape. Though the Home Depot was only a few miles away, he didn't want to have to carry a sheet of plywood home.

He climbed inside the truck and held out a face mask and pair of gloves to Derrick. They both put them on, then Derrick turned on the engine and pulled away from the curb.

As they drove out of their neighborhood, Matt was struck by how quiet everything was. No one was outside on this beautiful April morning. But even more striking was the lack of cars. Normally there would have been moderate traffic. It was spooky.

"Weird that no cars are on the road," Matt said.

"Yeah," Derrick said.

"When was the last time you were out of our neighborhood?" Matt glanced at Derrick, then went back to looking out his window.

"I guess about five days ago. When I figured out how bad this flu was I decided to hunker down at home."

Matt turned and looked at Derrick. "With your family?"

Derrick smiled. "I'm single."

"Where are your parents?"

His jaw clenched. "Los Angeles. But, uh, last time I spoke to them, they were both sick."

They both knew what that meant. "I'm sorry."

Derrick nodded. Both men were quiet as they turned onto the road that led to Home Depot.

A block away from Home Depot Derrick pulled to the

curb and shut off the engine. "We should approach on foot," he said. "See what's what."

Matt nodded. Derrick had combat experience whereas Matt's experience was sitting in front of a computer pounding out code. Yeah, he'd defer to Derrick.

They climbed out of the truck and made their way to the parking lot, keeping close to the fence. The parking lot came into view. A handful of cars were parked there, but not a soul could be seen. Across the parking lot was a Best Buy electronics store. The glass doors that led inside were smashed.

Derrick did a chin lift in that direction. "Idiots looted an electronics store." He snorted a laugh. "Now they can stare at their big screen TVs that don't work." He shook his head and moved forward, keeping close to the building.

As they got closer to the sliding doors, they saw that they were smashed as well. Matt wondered what the looters had left. He hoped there would be at least one sheet of plywood. When they reached the doors, Derrick, who was leading, stopped. Matt stopped behind him. Then, with his pistol at the ready, Derrick stepped through the opening made by the broken glass.

After a brief hesitation, Matt followed. After the bright sun, the interior was dim, but with the skylights in the ceiling, he could still see well enough. Derrick had stopped just inside the door so Matt stopped beside him.

Home Depot was a home improvement enthusiast's dream, a giant warehouse with aisle after aisle of hardware, tools, and other supplies for repairs, construction, and any other project around the house. Matt's gaze swept the immediate area. It looked like looters had a made a mess of the store, throwing what they hadn't taken onto the floor.

As Matt frowned at the mess he felt Derrick tap his shoulder. He looked at Derrick who touched his ear. That's when Matt heard it. The sound of people doing something somewhere in the enormous store.

They weren't the only ones inside.

CHAPTER 26

Matt

Derrick motioned to the right, then he pointed at Matt and motioned to the left. With a nod, they split up, and as Matt moved to the left, he gripped his .45, keeping his finger off of the trigger but at the ready. The last thing he wanted was to shoot someone, but things were different now. Law and order had broken down. He would do what he had to do.

As he made his way down the main aisle, his ears strained to tell where the activity was coming from. He wasn't going to lie. He hoped Derrick would come across the person or people first. He was much better equipped to handle conflict. But Matt knew he had to learn. Things were only going to get tougher, and with law enforcement non-existent, he would have to up his skills to include defense.

"Toss that over here," he heard a man call out, followed by a loud thump.

How many were there? More than one, it seemed. And they were close.

Matt moved forward, and when he remembered the way Derrick had snuck up on him the night before, he kept his head on a swivel.

Movement caught his eye. He eased closer, peering around the end of an aisle.

Two men were at the other end loading a ladder onto a flatbed cart that was already filled with a variety of other items. Maybe they were like him, needing a few things to secure their homes. Harmless.

"What do you think you're doing?" a man said from right behind Matt, then Matt felt something cold and metal pressed into the base of his skull. This time it wasn't someone's fingers.

Squeezing his eyes closed, Matt's first thought was that Derrick was going to kill him for not having enough situational awareness. But he'd been paying attention, so how had this man snuck up on him? And how dangerous was he?

"Drop your gun," the man said.

Matt had almost forgotten he was holding his .45. Without arguing, he let it fall to the floor.

"Kick it away from you."

He did.

"Now, turn around slowly and keep your hands where I can see 'em."

This man was all business. Would he shoot him?

Heart slamming against his ribs—*where was Derrick?* —Matt slowly turned to see a man who looked to be in his forties, slightly overweight with short hair and glasses. Not your typical bad guy. The man pointed his gun at Matt. "Why are you spying on us?"

All Matt could see was the huge black barrel aimed directly at him. He imagined the bullet coming straight out and killing him instantly. Terror wound its way up his throat and he found it hard to push words past his teeth.

The man jerked the gun toward him. "Answer me!"

"I…I need some plywood."

The man furrowed his brow and tilted his head. "What?"

Now that he'd found his voice, he felt his confidence growing. "I need a sheet of plywood. That's all." *Where was Derrick?!*

Using his gun, the man gestured to another part of the store. "You're in the wrong department." He chuckled at his own joke before adding, "I ought to shoot you right now." He laughed and the sound was filled with menace. "This here is the Wild West. I can do whatever I want and there's no one to stop me." The man spit on the ground at Matt's feet. "Least of all you."

"I don't want any trouble," Matt said. "Just a sheet of plywood."

The man squinted at him. "What do you need it for?"

He didn't want to get into a conversation about how his house had been broken into. "I just do. Now, if you'll excuse me."

The man laughed. "No, I won't excuse you. In fact, I think you need to meet some friends of mine. You can tell us all about where you're from, who else is in your group, what supplies you have. That kind of thing."

No way was Matt going to do that. He shook his head, but before he had a chance to open his mouth, the man jammed his gun against Matt's forehead. "I hope you weren't about to refuse. We don't take kindly to those who don't cooperate."

"Who you talking to, Will?" one of the men called out.

The man holding Matt hostage—Will—looked in the direction of his buddies, who were on the next aisle over. "I got it handled."

That's when Derrick came out of nowhere, slamming the butt of his gun into Will's head. Will crumpled to the floor.

Matt exhaled, his heart hammering wildly, and when Derrick looked meaningfully at Matt's gun lying on the floor, Matt snatched it from the ground.

Derrick zip-tied Will's hands behind his back, then lifted Will by the shoulders and looked at Matt with raised eyebrows. Feeling like he was slow on the uptake, Matt hustled over to Will, grabbing him by the ankles and helping Derrick carry the man to an area several aisles over.

Once they dropped him off, Derrick whispered, "There are two more. You take one and I'll take the other."

Did Derrick expect him to take one of the men down? Matt's eyes widened, but before he could protest, Derrick trotted away to approach the men from another direction and Matt was left trying to figure out what to do next.

It didn't take him long.

"Will!" one of the men called out. "Get over here!" When no one replied, Matt heard the man growl, "Go get him."

Knowing everything was about to hit the fan, Matt hurried to the end of the aisle where he would be hidden from view but would still be able to see the man who'd been sent to fetch Will.

"He's not here," the man called out.

No one replied. The man looked slightly worried as he turned in the direction he'd come from. "Ollie?"

Derrick must have done his part by taking out Ollie and now it was Matt's turn. He watched the man, whose face was clouding with alarm. The man turned this way and that before freezing in place, evidently listening, his back to Matt.

Time for Matt to make his move.

Quieter than he'd ever been in his life, Matt crept into the aisle and toward the man, who was about twenty feet away. As he got closer he saw that the man held a pistol in his right hand. Terrified that the man would see him before he'd gotten close enough to neutralize him, and that the man would then shoot *him*, Matt found it hard to put one foot in front of the other. Especially since his legs were trying to turn him around and go the other way, to safety.

But he had to do this. He had to prove not only to Derrick but to himself that he had the guts to do what had to be done. The first man, Will, had been more than willing to shoot Matt, had plainly stated that he could do whatever he wanted. Did his buddies feel the same way? Matt could only assume so.

Five feet away. Three feet.

The man turned, and the moment his eyes met Matt's, they widened with panic. The man dropped his gun and that's when Matt realized he was pointing his .45 at the man.

"On the ground," Matt said, surprised at how calm he felt. "Face down."

The man dropped to the floor and pressed his cheek to the cold concrete.

"Hands behind your back," Matt said. *Crap!* He didn't have a zip tie. Where was Derrick? Moments later he came around the corner wearing a grin. Derrick looked at the man on the floor and at Matt standing over him and nodded with approval, then handed a zip tie to Matt, who put it around the man's wrists.

"Found some rope," Derrick said before tossing it to Matt.

"What do you want me to…" He let his words trail off. Duh. The man needed to be tied to something so that he didn't run out of the place and get help to chase Matt and Derrick down.

After Matt secured the man to the shelving unit that was bolted to the floor, he turned to Derrick with a smile. "Let's go shopping."

By the time they left, they'd gathered a number of supplies, including the vegetable seed packets Jessica had requested, along with potting soil and seed starting trays.

Derrick brought his truck right up to the front entrance where they loaded everything up. Before they drove off, they checked on the three men they'd tied up. All three were spitting mad, swearing and threatening Matt and Derrick, but besides a bump on the heads of two of the men, they were okay.

As they walked toward the exit, Matt spoke quietly. "Should we have cut the zip ties?"

Derrick laughed. "If they're smart, they'll figure how to get loose."

Glad he hadn't had to shoot anyone, Matt worried that the time would come when he would have to kill or be killed. He was just grateful it hadn't been that day.

CHAPTER 27

Jessica

Jessica wished she'd suggested Matt take the walkie talkie with him. That way she could at least try to contact him. He'd been gone for hours, and as each minute ticked by, her worry multiplied.

A knock on the door startled her.

Leaping to her feet, she raced to the front window to see if she could tell who it was. A woman holding a handful of flyers walked across her lawn and to the neighbor's house.

"Who was that?" Kayla asked as she joined her mother at the window. Brooke was right behind her.

Jessica watched the woman until she was out of sight. "Someone dropping off flyers."

"Do you want me to get it?" Kayla asked.

"No," Jessica said as she turned to her daughter with a smile. She placed a hand on her arm. "I'll get it." Then, after putting on gloves, she went to the front door and opened it a crack. A flyer fluttered to the floor.

Jessica picked it up, noticing it was written by hand, which made sense since computers and printers would no longer work. Then she closed and locked the door.

"What's it say?" Kayla asked.

Jessica read it out loud. "Neighborhood meeting to discuss an important matter. 6PM at the school." She looked at Kayla. "I wonder what the important matter is."

Kayla shrugged. "Are we going to go?"

"Go where?" Dylan asked as he walked into the room, then he pointed to the flyer. "What's that?"

Jessica read it to him.

"Maybe it has something to do with that man who tried to break in," Brooke said.

Jessica nodded. "You're probably right."

"Then we should definitely go," Kayla said.

"What about Dad?" Dylan asked.

Which reminded Jessica of her worry. She glanced at her watch—she'd had to dig it out of her dresser since she hadn't worn it in ages. She'd become dependent on her phone to tell her the time and had stopped wearing it.

It was nearly two o'clock.

Trying to reassure the kids as much as herself, she said, "I'm sure Dad will be home soon. We'll see what he says."

Forty-five minutes later, Matt and Derrick arrived.

The moment she heard Derrick's truck, she looked heavenward in gratitude, then she raced outside to make sure Matt was okay. Then, to her surprise, she found him more than okay. He was in a fantastic mood. As soon as he stepped out of the truck, she threw her arms around him. "I've been so worried."

He kissed her soundly. "I'm home now. And I figured out a solution to our security problem."

His enthusiasm was contagious. "Oh yeah? What?"

Grinning, he said, "Take a look at these." He went to the bed of the truck and opened the tailgate. A number of black steel window security bars were stacked inside.

"Oh! That's perfect." Thrilled that they would have a way to secure their home, relief and calm flowed over her. "That means we can all go to tonight's meeting."

Matt tilted his head. "What meeting?"

"We got a flyer a little while ago that said there's a meeting at six tonight to discuss an important matter." Jessica glanced at Derrick, who stood nearby. "Do you think it has something to do with our break-in last night?"

Derrick nodded. "Probably."

"Then we'd better get busy and get these installed," Matt said. He looked at Dylan, who'd joined them at the curb. "Carry these in the house for me, will you?"

Dylan got right to work, then Matt took a small box from the truck's back seat and held it out to Jessica. "Your seeds."

She didn't know why she'd thought of asking him to get them at the last minute, but she was glad she had. Now they could plant a garden. She took the box and held it like the treasure it was. "Thank you." Then a new thought occurred to her. "Was anyone working there? I mean, were you able to pay for this stuff?" She kind of doubted any employees would be that loyal, but she had to know.

"Uh, not exactly."

"What do you mean? Did you just...take everything?"

"The world's changed," Derrick said as he hefted three security bar sets out of the truck and onto one shoulder. "We would have paid if we could have, but the place was abandoned." Then he glanced at Matt like there was something he wasn't saying.

She waited to see if Derrick would say more, but when he didn't she decided she would ask Matt about it later. Right now they needed to secure their home. And as far as not being able to pay for the things they'd taken, what else were they supposed to do? Their family's safety had to be their top priority.

"I need to charge up my drill," Matt said.

Remembering their decision not to advertise that they had a source of power, Jessica looked at Matt. One side of his mouth tugged up. "I told Derrick about the RV's solar panel."

"Your secret's safe with me," Derrick said with a chuckle.

Derrick had done so much to help her family that Jessica couldn't begrudge him knowing. "If you need to use it," she said, "you're welcome to."

"Thanks. I'll keep that in mind." He turned away, carrying the three sets of security bars into their house.

Jessica helped Matt bring in the rest of the items, then after thanking Derrick, who left, she fixed something for her family to eat while Matt took his drill out to the RV to charge it up.

After their meal, Jessica watched as Matt and Dylan affixed the security bars to all of the windows on the first floor and the basement. Meant to be secured from inside the house, they had hinges that allowed them to be swung open if access to the window was needed.

"It will be a lot harder for someone to break in now," Matt said as he latched the steel bars covering the front window.

"It looks like we live in a prison," Kayla said with disdain.

Matt scowled. "Would you rather have someone take all of our food?"

"No," she quickly said. "I just meant... Never mind." She shook her head and walked away.

"She never watched The Walking Dead," Dylan said with complete seriousness, "so she doesn't know how it is."

"How what is?" Jessica asked.

Dylan turned to her. "How people can get. What people will do for food." Then he grimaced. "At least we don't have walkers. That's what they call the zombies on The Walking Dead."

Holding back a laugh, Jessica nodded. "I know. I've seen a few episodes." She couldn't dispute what he'd said. People *did* do desperate and terrible things to get food. She just hoped they wouldn't have to deal with that.

CHAPTER 28

Matt

At a few minutes before six, Matt and his family left their house and walked the half mile to the elementary school for the neighborhood meeting. Now that all of his windows had been secured, he felt relatively comfortable leaving the house unguarded.

When they arrived at the school, a fair number of people were already there. Many, like his family, wore something over their noses and mouths. When he saw Tony talking to people at the front of the crowd, he was certain Tony had put the meeting together. He didn't see Charlie though, so he wondered if this meeting actually had anything to do with the break-in.

"Welcome," Tony said a few minutes later. The crowd quieted. Tony's gaze swept the assembled group. "I hate to say it, but I think there are fewer people here than we had at yesterday's meeting. Does anyone know if there were new…deaths?"

No one said anything, but everyone looked around.

"I was hoping the virus was petering out," he said, "but my hope may have been premature."

Matt frowned behind his face mask. He'd been hoping the same thing, but since it looked like the virus was still active, he was glad he'd had his family wear protective masks.

"I think my neighbor got sick," one man offered. "He was outside earlier today, coughing, and he's not here now."

Tony shook his head. "Has anyone, uh, checked on their neighbors to see their status?"

Matt, like everyone else, shook his head. No one was willing to risk their lives to check on their neighbors.

"Okay," Tony said, "let's move on." He cleared his throat then nodded at a man who Matt recalled was one of the three men who was ex-military. "Chris," Tony said. Chris walked away, going to an SUV parked along the curb. Everyone watched as Chris opened the rear door of the SUV and pulled another man out of the back seat. It was Charlie.

Most in the crowd gasped. Had they heard about the break-in attempt?

Matt felt Jessica's hand slip into his. He gently squeezed to let her know everything would be okay.

"So," Dylan murmured beside him, "it is going to be about that guy."

"Told ya," Brooke said.

Everyone watched with rapt attention as Chris led Charlie to stand near Tony.

"You may be wondering why this man is handcuffed," Tony began. A number of heads nodded. "I'll tell you why." He pointed at Charlie. "This man, Charles Swenson, was caught attempting to break in to an occupied home."

A low murmur filled the air.

Matt was glad Tony hadn't mention that it had been *his* home that had been involved. He didn't want to get dragged into this.

"Charles confessed that he'd planned it," Tony went on, "waiting until the husband and father would be away before he struck, breaking a window in his attempt. He was only stopped because men on patrol caught him in the act."

The murmur of the crowd grew louder.

"Tonight," Tony said with dramatic flair, "it is up to you to decide what should happen to Charles."

"Why'd you do it?" someone called out.

Tony turned to Charlie. "What do you have to say for yourself?"

Charlie shifted from one foot to the other, his gaze glued to the blacktop in front of him. Finally, he looked up, his eyes beseeching. "I'm sorry for what I did. I know it was wrong. My family..." His chin quivered. "They're starving. I was...I was desperate, but I was afraid to go into any of the houses with dead bodies in them. I mean, they still have the virus, right?"

"That's no excuse," one man shouted.

"Give him a break," a woman said.

"Why didn't you ask for help?" another man asked.

"So, you admit it?" a man near the front of the crowd asked.

Charlie looked at the ground again as he silently nodded.

"Since law enforcement is non-existent," Tony said, "it is up to us to decide what to do with him." He paused. "Before you decide, keep in mind that your decision will set a precedent for any future crimes in our neighborhood."

"We should help him," a woman said.

"You go right ahead," a man somewhere in the middle said, "and when your food is gone, don't come crying to me."

No one else suggested giving their food to feed Charlie's family.

Though Matt felt sorry for the man and his family, there were other options—trading, bargaining, scavenging. But outright stealing couldn't be tolerated. Especially when it had put his family in danger.

"What if we pool all of our resources?" a man shouted. "We could divide it among the neighborhood."

"Spoken like someone who has nothing to lose and everything to gain," another man shouted.

"I think that's a good idea," a woman said.

Tony nodded. "Okay. Those who vote for pooling our resources, raise your hands."

About one third of the people raised their hands.

"All right," Tony said. "Those of you who voted yes

ought to get together and pool your resources to distribute among yourselves."

"But we're almost out of food," one of the women who'd raised her hand said.

"Right," a man shouted. "Which is exactly why you want those of us who were prepared to contribute."

Everyone was silent. Clearly, that's exactly what they wanted.

Matt shook his head. What a mess. And it was only going to get worse as more and more people ran out of food. Including his family. They should be okay for quite a while, but eventually they would be in the same boat as those who'd already run out.

"We've gotten off track," Tony said. "What do we do with Charles here?"

"Banish him from the neighborhood," one man suggested.

Charlie's head snapped up. "You can't do that. I live here just like you."

"But we didn't try to rob our neighbor," the man who'd made the suggestion shot back.

"Are you saying you'd let your family starve?" Charlie asked, evidently no longer sorrowful for his crime. "You'd do nothing while you watched them die?"

No one replied to that. Matt wondered what he would do in that situation if it came to it. If there was no other way to feed his family, would he steal?

Yeah, he would. He would do anything. He figured most everyone else had reached the same conclusion. But he wasn't there yet. And he didn't want a desperate man living in their neighborhood. A man who, for all he knew, would attempt another break-in, but next time he might bring a weapon. No, he couldn't let that happen. He and his family had been a target once. He couldn't let that happen again. Not knowingly.

"I second the motion to banish him," Matt said in a loud voice.

Everyone turned to look at him.

"What gives you the right?" the woman who wanted to pool resources said with a scowl.

Hesitating, but only for a moment, he said, "Because my house is the one he tried to break in to. He broke one of my windows which now leaves me and my family vulnerable. He waited—*waited*—until my family was alone before he struck. He *planned* the break-in. It was pre-mediated. If we let him stay, you," he pointed to random people as he spoke, "could be next."

That got their attention and several other people agreed that Charlie should be made to leave the neighborhood.

"All in favor or banishing Charles from the neighborhood," Tony said, "raise your hand."

Eighty percent of the hands went up.

Tony nodded. "You will be escorted out of the neighborhood."

"What about my family?" Charlie asked.

"They may stay if they choose." He paused. "I'll personally make sure they get some food."

A look of incredulity swept over Charlie's face. "You're making me leave them?"

"No. They can go with you. But they don't have to."

Fury replaced the incredulity. "This is so wrong."

"Nevertheless, it is the decision of our people. Breaking in to an occupied house will not be tolerated."

Tony gestured with his chin to Chris, who grabbed Charlie by the upper arm and marched him back to the SUV.

"Wow," Dylan said.

Matt agreed. A week earlier something like this would have been unheard of.

Once Charlie had been led away, Tony faced the crowd. "Does anyone have any other concerns they need to discuss?"

No one said a word. Perhaps they were all in shock at the sudden and final verdict that they'd been a part of.

"Okay," Tony said. "Thank you for coming." At that, he turned away from the crowd and began speaking to someone nearby.

Matt turned to Jessica. "I guess that's it."

Her forehead was furrowed.

"What's wrong?"

"It's just..." She shook her head. "I don't know. How can we banish someone from their own home? It doesn't seem right."

Matt thought about the abject panic he'd felt when he'd heard glass breaking at his house mere hours earlier. He hadn't known if his family was hurt or what was going on.

That couldn't be allowed. "Do you remember how scared you were when you called me on the walkie talkie late last night?"

Jessica nodded. "Yeah."

"If we're lenient with Charlie, then what's to stop the next guy from wanting to try the same thing? And the next guy might actually be good at what he's doing. He might get in and hurt you or the kids."

"You're right." She was quiet a moment. "I guess I just have to get used to this new world where people do things they wouldn't normally do."

Matt thought about what had happened at Home Depot. How the man—Will—had held a gun to his head and had threatened to kill him. How he'd said they lived in the Wild West now. Should he tell Jessica about that?

One look at the fear and confusion in her eyes and he knew this wasn't the time.

CHAPTER 29

Jessica

Over the next twenty-four hours things were calm and Jessica almost began to believe that everything was going to be okay, that everything would somehow work out. Then, in the afternoon, a flyer was delivered to their door.

Matt got it and brought it inside, scowling as he read it over.

"What's wrong?" she asked as fresh worry splashed over her.

He held up the flyer. "Says there's a meeting in," he looked at his watch, "one hour. And every family who comes is required to bring one food item to donate to the 'Neighborhood Cooperative.'" He did air quotes at that.

"Neighborhood cooperative? Since when do we have a neighborhood cooperative?" Jessica had a bad feeling. She remembered the number of people at the meeting the day before who'd wanted to pool everyone's resources. Was this tied to that?

"We don't have a neighborhood cooperative as far as I know," Matt said with a frown. "Besides, we already gave some food to those three families."

"What's going on?" Dylan asked as he joined them in the family room.

Matt handed him the flyer. Dylan read it then tilted his head in question. "Weird." Then he looked at Matt. "Are you guys going?"

Jessica was wondering the same thing.

Matt looked at her. "What do you think?"

"Maybe we should. Just to find out what this is all about."

He nodded. "I agree. Pick out a can of something we have plenty of and we'll head over in a bit."

Fifty minutes later, wearing their usual earloop masks, she and Matt walked out the door and toward the school. When they got there, they set the can of green beans in a box that had about a dozen other items in it.

"Thank you," a man standing beside the box said with a grateful smile.

Knowing he or his family was probably in need, she felt better about the donation. "You're welcome."

When it was time for the meeting to start, there were around twenty-five people there. A dozen fewer than had been at the meeting the day before. Was that because people didn't want to bring food—or didn't have any—or because they were sick? Hoping it was the former, Jessica looked around for Tony but didn't see him.

"I wonder where Tony is," she murmured to Matt.

He lifted his shoulders in a shrug.

A man they'd seen at other meetings stepped to the front of the group. "Thank you all for coming." He glanced at the box of donated food items before facing the group. "And thank you for your donations."

"Where's Tony?" someone called out.

The man leading the meeting glanced at the man who'd thanked Jessica and Matt for the food when they'd arrived, then he looked at the man who'd asked the question. "I'm afraid I have bad news."

Jessica felt her insides clench.

"Tony, uh, he passed away earlier today."

Now her heart pounded. Someone she'd really liked had died. It was so pointless and tragic.

Murmured voices filled the air.

The man who'd announced Tony's passing waited until everyone had settled down, then with a grim smile, said, "My name's Eric Lawson. I'm the one who called today's meeting."

Intensely interested to see what this meeting was about, Jessica waited to hear what Eric had to say.

"Do you see Derrick?" Matt whispered beside her.

Jessica looked at everyone, then shook her head. "No."

He'd been at the other meetings. Interesting that he hadn't come to this one.

Jessica pictured him getting sick. Her heart skipped a

beat. Derrick had helped them so much, the thought of him getting sick and dying made her heart hurt.

"Maybe he's busy," she said. "Or maybe he didn't see the flyer in time." After all, they'd only gotten it an hour earlier.

"Yeah," Matt said.

"The reason I called this meeting," Eric said, then he glanced at five men who stood near him like they were all in on whatever was about to happen, "is to discuss our new neighborhood cooperative." Jessica recognized one of the men—Chris. He was the one who'd led Charlie to and from the SUV the day before.

"Cooperative," someone shouted, "what cooperative?"

Jessica wondered the same thing.

"In light of what happened with that break-in the other day, I know many of you are concerned about security. But there are more serious security concerns." He looked at Bryant Johnson, the man with the Ham radio. "Bryant, what is the latest news on that front?"

All eyes swiveled in Bryant's direction. "There have been reports of gangs going into neighborhoods, house to house, taking what they want. Killing anyone who resists."

Stunned at the news, Jessica felt shivers race up her spine. It was bad enough that Charlie had attempted to break in. He'd been an amateur. The thought of armed gangs, on the other hand, terrified her. Especially with two teenaged girls to protect.

Jessica turned to Matt, who was completely focused on what Bryant was saying.

"How close to our neighborhood?" someone asked.

"A couple of miles at most."

"Thank you, Bryant," Eric said, drawing everyone's attention back to him. His gaze swept the group. "We all have families to protect, but nothing in life is free. Not before this virus and certainly not now. Especially not now. So, what the cooperative decided is, if you want the benefit of neighborhood-provided security, you need to join our cooperative." He paused as loud voices filled the air.

"You decided?" someone shouted.

"This can't be good," Matt said beside Jessica. She nodded as a feeling of foreboding washed over her.

Eric held up his hands. After several minutes everyone quieted down.

"I'm sure you're all wondering what this cooperative is all about," he said. "We will explain." He turned to one of the men who'd been standing to the side and nodded to him. The man stepped forward.

"I'm Russ Givens, chairman of the Neighborhood Cooperative."

"Hold on," one man shouted. "When did this cooperative form and who put you in charge?"

Russ smirked. "A group of us got together and organized it, got agreements from security and medical personnel to work for us, then decided to invite the entire neighborhood to join."

This was sounding more and more ominous to Jessica, but she kept quiet as she waited to hear what they had in mind.

"How does it work?" a woman called out.

Russ smiled. "I'm about to explain." He paused dramatically. "Everyone who joins the cooperative will have access to security and medical care." He gestured to Chris. "Chris Jackson, who has combat experience, will head up our security team." He faced the group again. "Dr. Larsen, who is home treating patients, will head medical."

On its face it sounded good, but Jessica knew there was a catch. She turned to Matt, who looked at her with raised eyebrows.

CHAPTER 30

Matt

Matt waited for the other shoe to drop. There was no way this cooperative would offer their perks without wanting something in return. And he had a feeling he knew what it was.

"How do we join?" someone asked.

"I'm glad you asked," Russ said like a used car salesman. "Anyone is welcome to join. In fact, we hope the entire neighborhood will join." He grinned in a smarmy way. "The more the merrier."

Matt wondered if Russ had actually been a used car salesman.

"Like I said before," Russ continued, "members of our neighborhood cooperative will have full access to medical care and security—two things that are vital in this world." He paused. "Well, just like in the world we've always known, people who provide services need to get paid for those services."

Here it comes.

"That payment will come in the form of food donations to the co-op."

Of course.

"However," Russ said with what was probably supposed to pass as a compassionate smile, "we know that not everyone has much to give." He paused dramatically. "Which is why your payment will be based on what you have rather than a flat fee that is the same for everyone."

A deep sense of unease settled over Matt.

"How will you decide how much we need to pay?" a woman asked.

"A member of the committee will take an inventory of your food and then tell you how much you're required to pay."

"No way," several people shouted as others said, "Forget that." "Uh-uh."

"What if we refuse?" someone asked.

Eric stepped forward. "That's certainly your right, but if you're not a member of the neighborhood cooperative then our security and medical services won't be available to you."

Anger burned a trail up Matt's throat. It was extortion, plain and simple.

"That's not right," a woman cried out.

Russ laughed. "It's the American way."

"It's mob tactics," Matt heard himself yell. "Protection

for payment. And if we don't pay, are *you* going to rob us?" He pointed at Russ and Eric and the other men who stood with them.

Outrage swept across their faces, but Matt noticed that Chris also looked like he felt some guilt and discomfort.

Russ pointed at Bryant. "Didn't you hear what Bryant just said? Gangs are only a couple of miles from our neighborhood. Are you willing to risk your family's safety? What are you going to do if gangs break down your door and take *all* of your food? And worse? Then you'll wish you'd given a tiny portion of your food to the cooperative because then you'd be safe."

Matt scowled beneath his face mask. Even if people joined this cooperative, there was no guarantee their security people would get there in time. Even in the old world, law enforcement wasn't always there at the exact moment they were needed. And that was when there was a way to call them.

"How can members of this co-op let you know when they need help?" Matt asked.

Russ turned to Chris. "We'll let our head of security answer that."

Chris, who looked to be in his early thirties with broad shoulders and a confident demeanor, stepped forward. "There will be round-the-clock patrols so a security team will always be close by."

"Thank you, Chris," Russ said with a self-assured swagger. Then he faced the crowd. "Any other questions?"

"What if we don't have any food to give?" a man asked.

"There's room for everyone in our cooperative. We would just need to find a way for you to contribute in another way." Russ lifted his gaze to take in the entire crowd. "If your family would like to join the neighborhood cooperative, come see us and we'll get your name and address and schedule a time for a committee member to stop by and talk to you in your home."

Letting these people into his home was the *last* thing Matt would allow. He turned to Jessica. "Let's go." He began walking away with Jessica beside him, and as they passed through the gathering, others began leaving, but there were many who were telling Eric and Russ that they wanted to join the co-op.

Shaking his head in disgust, Matt knew he needed to find Derrick and tell him about this latest development.

After making sure Jessica made it safely home, Matt got on his bicycle to ride to Derrick's house. He didn't want to waste the fuel in his truck. There was no telling if he and his family would need to leave the neighborhood, but if they did, he wanted to be able to get as far as possible before his diesel ran out.

Derrick lived several streets over. Matt hadn't been there before and he only knew Derrick's address because Derrick had told him the day before. Now, as he approached Derrick's house on his bike, he saw Derrick's truck parked in the driveway. Leaning his bike against Derrick's garage, Matt took a deep breath before approaching the house. He didn't know what kind of security Derrick had set up—although he was certain he would have some.

Walking quietly, although not sneaking, he made his way up the walkway from the driveway to the front door. When he reached the door, he knocked firmly and called out, "It's Matt."

The door swung open.

"Hey," Derrick said, one hand pressed to the side of his right leg.

Matt's gaze went to the gun held there, and when Derrick tucked the firearm into the holster at his waist, Matt relaxed.

Derrick grinned. "Can't be too careful." Then he stepped back, allowing Matt to enter. "What brings you by?"

Matt crossed the threshold. "You need to hear about the meeting I just went to."

Derrick closed the door with a frown. "I know all about it."

Surprised that Derrick had known but hadn't come, especially to a meeting that would have such an impact on the neighborhood, Matt raised his eyebrows. "You missed a doozy."

A muscle worked in Derrick's jaw. "So, they're going ahead with it?"

Confused, Matt frowned. "You know about the co-op?"

Derrick gestured to his living room. Moments later they were seated across from each other.

Derrick scowled. "Russ and Eric came to me earlier today to see if I'd head up their new security division."

Shocked, Matt said, "I take it you turned them down."

Derrick chuckled. "You could say that."

"What happened?"

"They offered me a nice deal. Head up security in exchange for all the food and supplies I would need."

"A guy named Chris Jackson is heading it up."

That seemed to surprise Derrick. "Is that so?"

"Yeah. Do you know him?"

"Sure do."

"Dr. Larsen is part of it too."

Derrick shook his head. "I wonder if they approached Jeff."

"Jeff?"

"Yeah. He's military too." He chuckled. "Interesting that they approached both me and Chris. I've gotta assume they asked Jeff." Derrick narrowed his eyes. "Was Jeff at the meeting?"

"Now that you mention it, no."

"Huh."

"There's something else."

Tilting his head, Derrick said, "What?"

"Tony's dead."

Derrick recoiled slightly, then he looked thoughtful. "Interesting."

"Why do you say that?"

He chewed on his lip. "Don't you find it coincidental that he was healthy yesterday, but the same day this cooperative is announced, he's dead?"

What was Derrick suggesting? Some sort of foul play? If that was the case, what were these people capable of?

"Yeah," Matt said after thinking it over. "It is." When Derrick didn't say anything, Matt asked, "What are you thinking?"

Derrick stood. "We need to check on something."

We? "Okay." After what Derrick had done for him at Home Depot, Matt couldn't exactly refuse.

The two of them walked out the front door. Derrick glanced at Matt's bike with a smirk, then they climbed into Derrick's truck. Less than a minute later they pulled to the curb in front of a house with a bright red X painted on the front door. Nervous about going anywhere near an infected body, Matt stared at Derrick. "Whose house is this?"

Looking toward the house, then at Matt, Derrick said, "Tony's."

The body would be fresh. Perfect.

"And we're here because?"

Derrick laughed. "I just have a feeling."

Tilting his head, Matt said, "Does this feeling include a concern that you'll catch the virus that is killing pretty much everyone who gets it?"

"Nope." He opened the door and stepped onto the pavement.

"This guy's nuts," Matt muttered, then he got out of the truck. "Guess I am too."

"What's that?" Derrick said as he strode to the front door.

"Nothing." He was just glad he was wearing his mask. He pulled a pair of latex gloves out of his pocket and tugged them on.

CHAPTER 31

Matt

The paint forming the X was obviously fresh—only hours old—a thick drip of red trailing down the cheerful turquoise-colored door.

Derrick knocked, then he turned to Matt with an embarrassed smile. "Guess no one's going to answer."

Matt remembered that Tony had said his entire family had died of the virus. "Right."

Derrick took hold of the knob, but it didn't turn. "Locked," he said with a frown. He took a step back before landing a solid kick on the deadbolt. It took two more kicks before the door broke open.

The stench hit them immediately.

"Huh," Derrick said, but Matt wanted to hurl.

"Do you find something about the smell interesting?" Matt asked, nearly gagging. They hadn't stepped inside yet and the body wasn't in sight.

"Yeah. If Tony died within the last few hours, I wouldn't expect there to be such an awful smell yet."

"They said he died earlier today."

Derrick turned and looked at him. "He was alive at the meeting yesterday afternoon."

"True."

Derrick stepped over the threshold. Matt reluctantly followed.

As they went deeper into the house, the stink increased. Matt threw his hand over the mask covering his nose and mouth and breathed through his mouth. It didn't help.

"I think he's in here," Derrick said as they approached a closed door at the end of a hallway.

Matt braced himself. Even with all the dead and dying, he had yet to see a corpse.

Derrick opened the door. Matt's gaze shot to the figure crumpled on the floor next to the bed. It was Tony. But something wasn't right. Did people with the virus bleed out before they died? Because blood was everywhere.

"Just as I suspected. Tony didn't die of the flu," Derrick stated. "He was murdered."

Stunned that their suspicions were accurate, Matt felt his heart do a kind of ker-thump. This was bad. Very, very bad.

Derrick pointed to the lamp lying on the floor beside Tony. It was covered in blood. "Someone beat him to death."

Sickened by the sight in front of him as well as the idea that this cooperative—if they were responsible—were capable of this, Matt just stared with his mouth hanging open.

Derrick gestured with his head that they should leave. Matt eagerly led the way out the front door. Gulping in fresh air with a greed he'd never known before, he waited for Derrick to follow, but he didn't come out for another thirty seconds. When he did, he closed the broken door as best he could before leading the way to his truck where they both got in. It wasn't until they'd pulled away from the curb that Derrick spoke. "His pantry was empty. Completely empty."

Matt remembered Bryant talking about gangs that were taking what they wanted and killing anyone who resisted. Maybe it wasn't the cooperative at all. Maybe it was one of those gangs. Matt voiced his thoughts.

"No," Derrick said with a certainty that surprised Matt. "It was the co-op."

"What makes you so sure?"

"Think about it, Matt. Yesterday when someone suggested pooling resources, Tony said that those who wanted to pool resources should go ahead and do it and leave everyone else out of it. If this co-op came to him with the idea you heard today, do you think he would have endorsed it?"

Derrick had a good point. "No."

"Exactly. Which is why they killed him. And as a bonus, they took whatever food he had."

The thought of Tony, a man Matt had grown to respect, being bludgeoned to death by the men at today's meeting because he wouldn't agree to their socialist plan made his blood boil.

"What should we do?" he asked.

"I haven't decided. I want to talk to Jeff first."

Matt didn't know the ex-military man, but if Derrick did, all the better. The more men with combat experience on their side, the better. Then again, Chris had combat experience and he'd aligned with the cooperative.

Moments later they were at Jeff's house. He was home, although he was busy cleaning the guns in his impressive collection. Matt marveled at the variety of firearms spread out on his dining room table. Fresh air breezed in from the open windows.

"I'd offer you something to eat," said Emily, his girlfriend, "but Jeff's put us on rations." She smirked in Jeff's direction.

"We're fine," Derrick said with a chuckle.

Matt nodded his agreement, then considered the idea of rationing food for his own family. At first it had felt like they had plenty of food, but with five mouths to feed their supplies were beginning to diminish. They hadn't broken out the freeze-dried food yet, but when they did, it wouldn't last forever.

"What's up?" Jeff said as he ran a bore brush back and forth through the barrel of the pistol he was cleaning. He wore a ball cap backwards on his head and it looked like he'd given up on shaving.

"Wanted to talk to you about the neighborhood cooperative."

Jeff stopped what he was doing and looked at Derrick with a furrowed brow. "Yeah. They asked me to join their security team but I told them what they could do with their little co-op." He went back to cleaning his weapon.

Matt held down a chuckle, glad these two men felt the same way about the cooperative as he did.

Derrick glanced at Matt before saying, "Jackson's heading up security for them."

That got Jeff's attention. He set down the bore brush and pistol and stood. The man was well over six feet. "You're kidding."

Derrick frowned. "Nope."

"This group is bad news," Matt added. Jeff needed to know what the cooperative was capable of.

Jeff turned to him. "I got that sense when they came by. Said they'd provide food for me. When I asked where they would get it, they said members of the cooperative would donate it." One side of his mouth quirked up. "I doubt those donations would be voluntary."

Matt told them what Russ had explained at the meeting. Then he glanced at Derrick before saying, "Looks like they don't tolerate resistance."

Jeff tilted his head. "What do you mean?"

Derrick became somber. "Tony's been murdered."

Surprise swept over Jeff's face. "Murdered?"

"Yeah. Matt and I went to his house before we came over. Found him bludgeoned to death."

Jeff stared at his array of weapons, then he looked at Derrick. "Not sure what you want me to do about it."

Derrick raised an eyebrow. "What if they come after you next?"

Tilting his head like that was ridiculous, Jeff said, "I'd like to see them try."

Matt knew he wouldn't want to go up against Jeff, but he was still surprised he didn't seem at least a little nervous.

Derrick just laughed. "Okay, bro. Thanks for the time."

"Sure thing." Jeff took a step toward the front door. Clearly, the meeting was over.

Disappointed that these guys weren't going to do something about the cooperative, Matt had no choice but to leave with Derrick. Once they were back in his truck, Matt said, "Now what?"

"Now we have a little chat with Chris Jackson."

CHAPTER 32

Matt

Maybe Derrick was going to do something about the cooperative. Then a new idea occurred to Matt. Was Chris the one who'd killed Tony? After all, he was the head of security.

Minutes later they were standing on Chris's front porch, talking to his wife, a woman in her early thirties with a toddler in her arms and a boy who was about six years old hiding behind her legs.

"Chris should be back any minute," she said as the little boy with blond hair wriggled in her arms. She set him down and he toddled off behind her.

Seeing her small children, Matt had a new understanding of why Chris may have agreed to be part of the cooperative. Surely they were going to give food to his family.

"How are things going, Amy?" Derrick asked.

Her shoulders slumped. "The truth? Not good. We're nearly out of food, and," she glanced behind her, "there are only a few diapers left." Then her face brightened. "But things are looking up. This neighborhood cooperative will be a huge blessing."

At whose expense? Matt wondered.

Derrick smiled tightly. "Right."

"Hey, Derrick," a friendly voice said from a distance behind them.

They turned to see Chris walking up the driveway toward the front door. As he reached them, they stepped back to allow him to pass. He kissed his wife, then turned to Matt and Derrick. "You were at today's meeting," he said to Matt.

"Yeah. I'm Matt Bronson."

"Chris Jackson." He hesitated, but only for a moment. "I have to say, people weren't pleased when you basically called the neighborhood cooperative the mafia."

Derrick turned to Chris with a chuckle. "Can you say you're not?"

Chris motioned to the chairs on the porch. "Let's talk."

It was a beautiful afternoon, and with no electricity, outside was better than in. The three of them settled into wicker chairs.

"You should know," Derrick began, "Russ and Eric came to see me this morning about heading security for their cooperative."

Chris stared at him. "You're saying I wasn't their first choice."

Derrick shook his head. "I have no idea. But that's not the point."

Scowling, Chris asked, "Then what is?"

"I turned them down for a reason."

"Uh-huh."

"Clearly, you felt differently."

Chris glanced toward his house. "I have a family, Derrick. A wife and two small children. We're almost out of food." He frowned. "I get an offer to feed my family? Of course I'm going to take it."

Matt couldn't fault him for doing what he believed was best for his family. The truth was, if Matt was nearly out of food, he'd probably join the cooperative too. But the reality was, he had food, but he didn't want to be coerced into giving it away at his family's expense.

Matt stared at Chris. "What happens if someone not in the cooperative needs help? Like, if you see someone being attacked by these roving gangs we heard about. Would you just stand by and watch?"

Chris shifted in his seat like he didn't want to have to deal with that. "I mean, of course not." Then his eyes cut to the side as if someone from the cooperative might have overheard.

Matt noticed the move. "What would happen if you did help someone not in the co-op and Russ or Eric found out?"

He shook his head. "No idea." Then he frowned, deeply. "Look. I'm just doing this to help my family, okay? I don't like the way it's dividing our neighborhood."

Derrick made a scoffing sound. "You're surprised that

happened? I mean, come on. People are going to be forced to give up their food just to keep their family safe? That's not right."

Grimacing, Chris said, "I didn't make the rules—"

"No," Matt said, cutting him off, "but you're benefiting from them. At the expense of those who are weaker than you."

Chris frowned at him. "I'm not gonna let my family starve because some people don't approve of my choices."

Why were he and Derrick there? Had Derrick hoped to change Chris's mind? Then he pictured Tony, crumpled in a pool of coagulated blood. "Did you kill Tony?"

Chris looked at Matt with wide eyes. Derrick frowned.

"What?" Chris asked. "No!"

"Someone did," Matt said. He looked at Derrick for backup. "We saw him. Someone beat him to death."

Chris looked at Derrick in stunned disbelief. "Is that true?"

Either Chris was a good actor or he was telling the truth.

"Yeah," Derrick said with a grimace. "It's true."

Then Chris turned on Matt. "Why in the world would you think *I* did it? You don't know me. I wouldn't kill a man in cold blood."

Matt had no idea who had killed Tony, but someone obviously had. It hadn't been the virus that had killed him. "You're head of security for this neighborhood cooperative."

Chris narrowed his eyes. "I still don't get the connection."

Was he being dense?

Derrick cleared his throat and both men turned to him. "The co-op had the motive."

Now Chris tilted his head like he didn't want to believe it. "Look, the people who organized the co-op are good people, just like you. I don't believe they would kill Tony—or anyone else."

Without law enforcement to process the crime scene, it was possible they would never know who had killed Tony. All Matt knew was that he would have to be on his guard. If a murderer was in their midst, none of them were safe.

Thinking about that led to thoughts of his family. He wanted to be with them. He stood. "I've gotta run."

"Yeah," Derrick said as he stood. "Me too. Thanks for talking with us, Chris."

Chris stood as well. "We've known each other for a while, Derrick. We may not agree on the cooperative, but that's not a reason to be enemies."

Derrick smiled. "Agree to disagree."

Chris nodded, then he turned to Matt. "Best of luck."

Matt didn't want any enemies. Especially not someone who could possibly step between danger and his family. Matt smiled. "You too."

Maybe he should give Chris and his family some of their precious food stores. Then again, he wouldn't be able to give them enough to keep them fed for long, and with the co-op already feeding them, what would be the point?

With a final nod, he and Derrick walked away.

CHAPTER 33

Jessica

Eager to plant the seeds Matt had picked up, first thing the next morning Jessica oversaw the family as they worked together to place the seeds in the seed starting boxes that Matt had gotten. It was April—too early in the season to plant outside—but if they got the starts going, they would be able to put the plants in the ground in a few more weeks.

Cleo kept nosing her way into the potting soil. Laughing, Jessica gently pushed her away.

"She loves to garden," Brooke said with a rare smile as she added a few drops of water to the soft soil of a tomato plant.

Lately, it seemed as if Brooke's melancholy wasn't as constant. Having Cleo helped tremendously.

Jessica scratched Cleo's head. "She's a good dog."

Once all the starts were done, they lined them up on a high table beside a south facing window.

"That should give them enough sun," Jessica said, "but soon it'll be warm enough to put them on the back patio."

"I think it's cool that we're growing our own food," Kayla said with a satisfied smile.

Jessica agreed. Now that they couldn't run to the store to get groceries, they were going to have to learn a new way of life. "Who's hungry for lunch?"

"I am," Dylan said.

"You know I can always eat," Matt said.

"We have two apples left," Jessica said. "After all our hard work this morning, let's celebrate by having those." She turned to Kayla. "Will you slice them up?"

Excitement filled her eyes. "Sure."

It made Jessica sad that the opportunity to eat an apple would bring her daughter so much joy. Before, Kayla probably would have said she didn't want it—she hadn't been the best about eating produce. It was too bad that it had taken something so drastic to make her children appreciate the things they used to take for granted.

Jessica worked on making sandwiches, using half of their remaining loaf of bread. What would they do once that was gone? Would she be able to get her hands on enough yeast and other ingredients to make her own? She'd never made her own bread before. Would she be able to figure out how to do it?

"Ow!" Kayla screamed from where she was working.

Jessica turned to see blood dripping from one of Kayla's

fingers. "Oh no." She grabbed the first aid kit they'd stashed in one of the kitchen cabinets. After pulling out a gauze pad, she wrapped it around Kayla's finger. "How bad do you think it is?"

Kayla grimaced. "I don't know, but it really hurts."

She put gentle pressure on the cut.

"What happened?" Matt asked as he joined them in the kitchen.

"Kayla cut her finger."

"Let me take a look," he said.

Kayla held out her hand and he carefully unwrapped the gauze.

"Looks pretty deep," Matt said. He looked at Jessica. "She might need stitches."

Kayla frowned. "Are the hospitals open?"

As far as Jessica knew, they were closed. She looked at Matt.

"I don't know," Matt said, "but Dr. Larsen should be able to take care of it."

Jessica looked at Matt sharply. At the meeting the day before, the people running the neighborhood cooperative had made it clear that only members of the cooperative could go to Dr. Larsen.

"Maybe we should check the hospital first," Jessica said. She didn't want trouble with the cooperative.

"If it's open it'll be filled with people who are infected with the virus."

She hadn't thought of that, but of course he was right.

They couldn't risk it. Not over a cut finger. "Okay. Can we go see Dr. Larsen now?"

Concern flashed across Matt's face, but he nodded. "Yeah." He wrapped the gauze back around Kayla's finger.

"Look at all that blood," Dylan said with obvious fascination.

Frowning, Jessica shooed him away. "Dad and I are going to get this taken care of. You and Brooke stay here."

"Okay," Dylan said.

Brooke nodded, then she smiled, "I'll keep him in line."

"Good luck with that," Kayla said with a grin.

Jessica walked with Matt and Kayla to the front door. "Are we driving?" she asked.

"Yeah. Dr. Larsen lives a few streets over."

As they drove to Dr. Larsen's house, Jessica worried about her agreeing to treat Kayla. She was a doctor, but when she found out they didn't belong to the cooperative, would she refuse?

A few moments later they arrived. A sign on Dr. Larsen's front door said she was open to patients and to come right in. The welcoming sign made Jessica feel better, and as she opened the door and crossed the threshold, she felt herself relaxing.

"Knock, knock," Jessica called out when she didn't see anyone.

"I'm back here," a female voice called out. "Come on back."

Jessica led the way to the family room at the back of the house where she saw Dr. Larsen wearing jeans and t-shirt. It wasn't the typical doctor's attire, but these weren't typical times.

"Hello," Jessica said. "Our daughter Kayla cut her finger." She motioned to Kayla, who looked a little pale.

Concern flitted across Dr. Larsen's face. "Oh no. Let me take a look." She led Kayla to a chair, and once she was seated, Dr. Larsen turned to Jessica and Matt. "What are your names?"

"Matt and Jessica," Matt said.

Dr. Larsen nodded, then said, "Would you please sign the register?" She pointed toward a binder lying open on the kitchen counter, then she turned her attention to Kayla.

While Dr. Larsen examined Kayla's finger, Jessica followed Matt to the binder. He picked up the pen, and without speaking, he pointed to the column headings. They read *Name, Address, Co-op Member #*. Then, with the pen resting on the last column heading, he looked at Jessica with raised eyebrows.

She bit her lip. They didn't have a member number. Was that going to be an issue?

Matt gently set the pen down and turned away from the register. Jessica's heart pounded. It felt like they were at the hospital with no insurance.

They stood with their backs to the binder and watched as Dr. Larsen cleaned the cut and expertly stitched it up. When she was done, she wrapped the finger in a fresh gauze bandage and smiled. Then she handed a bottle to Kayla. "These are antibiotics to prevent infection. Take two per day until they're gone."

"Thank you so much," Jessica said.

"Yes," Kayla said. "Thank you."

Before Dr. Larsen had a chance to look at the register and discover they hadn't filled it out, Jessica and Matt hurried Kayla out the door.

CHAPTER 34

Matt

As they drove home, Matt felt a little bit like a thief. He'd taken medical services from Dr. Larsen without giving her anything in return.

"Maybe we ought to bring Dr. Larsen some food or something," he said.

Jessica bit her lip. "What about giving her one of our first aid kits? We have several."

"Good idea."

After dropping Jessica and Kayla off and grabbing one of the small first aid kits, Matt drove back to Dr. Larsen's house, then walked inside. "Dr. Larsen?"

"I'm back here," she said.

With the first aid kit in hand, he walked into the family room. When she saw him, she frowned. "You didn't fill out the register earlier."

Maybe coming back had been a mistake. "Uh, yeah. We,

uh, we don't belong to the cooperative." He held out the first aid kit. "But I brought this as payment."

She looked at the first aid kit a moment before taking it from him. "Thank you. I can always use more medical supplies." She set it on the counter, then turned back to face him. "However, I will have to report this to the cooperative."

Well, crap. "Can't you just, you know, let it slide? This once?"

She smiled sadly. "I wish I could, but if they found out, it would be a problem for me."

An image of Tony with his skull bashed in filled Matt's mind. Had the cooperative threatened Dr. Larsen?

Knowing he couldn't stop her from telling them he'd been there, he softly sighed and shook his head, then he turned and left.

As he drove home it occurred to him that all Dr. Larsen knew about them were their first names. For all he knew, she wouldn't remember those and their family would manage to fly under the co-op's radar.

Just to be safe, when he got home, he told Jessica and the kids his concern, instructing them to lay low. Then he closed all the blinds. He wanted to be able to see any visitors before they saw him.

That afternoon a loud knock sounded at the front door. Cleo barked wildly.

"Do you think it's them?" Jessica whispered, wide-eyed, as they stood frozen in the living room.

Matt didn't know, but he feared that it was. "Let me see

what I can see." He went to the blinds covering the front window and lifted a slat slightly, peering out. Russ and Eric stood on the walkway in front of his door. He didn't see Chris, the head of security. Not sure if that was a good thing or a bad thing, he debated whether or not to open the door.

Dropping the slat back into place, he turned to Jessica, then looked at the kids, who had joined them in the living room. His gaze went to Kayla. Her finger was wrapped in gauze and was on its way to healing, thanks to Dr. Larsen. Maybe he could make a deal with the cooperative rather than join it.

"Let me handle this," he said. He glanced at Cleo. "Come, girl." He put on a face mask before going to the front door and pulling it open, letting Cleo stand beside him. He held her collar, but when she growled at the men, he didn't correct her. "Good afternoon." Neither man smiled, but Matt noticed them glancing at Cleo with nervous looks. Good. "What can I help you with?"

Russ focused on Matt. "We understand your family utilized Dr. Larsen's medical services. Is that correct?"

Should he deny it? He was certain these guys already knew the answer. Besides, if they saw the gauze bandage on Kayla's finger, they would know that they had.

Lifting his chin in defiance, Matt nodded once. "Yes."

Russ clenched his jaw and Eric's eyebrows rose like they were surprised he'd admitted it. Had they expected him to deny it?

Cleo seemed to calm, sitting beside Matt. He released her collar. If she lunged at the men, he wouldn't stop her.

"As you're aware," Russ said with a quick glance at Cleo, "only members of the neighborhood cooperative are allowed to go to Dr. Larsen."

The way he said it, like he was in charge of everything in the neighborhood, rubbed Matt the wrong way. Especially when there weren't other options for medical care. What was he supposed to do? Put a band-aid on a deep cut and hope his daughter didn't get an infection that could lead to her losing her finger, her hand, or even her life?

The more he thought about it, the angrier he became.

Forcing himself to remain calm, he said, "I disagree."

"You disagree? With what? The rule is the rule."

Normally Matt avoided confrontations, but this was ridiculous. It was time to tell these guys what was on his mind. Heart pounding, he said, "You may think you're in charge, but it's an illusion. No one's in charge anymore."

"Wrong," Russ said, his tone showing his absolute certainty, which just riled Matt up all the more. "We made a deal with Dr. Larsen."

"I already paid her," Matt said.

Russ laughed. "Yeah. She showed us that pitiful first aid kit."

It wasn't the biggest first aid kit, but Dr. Larsen had only spent about twenty minutes on Kayla. In this world, the payment had seemed generous.

"Since you used the co-op's medical services," Russ went on, "you're required to either join or make a payment we determine."

Even though it irked him, Matt wanted to try to resolve this amicably. "What payment do you have in mind?"

Russ tilted his head. "That depends."

Unease growing, Matt asked, "On what?"

"On what you have."

He narrowed his eyes. "What do you mean?"

"Eric and I will take a look at your supplies and determine payment."

Matt's hackles rose. "No."

Cleo must have felt the tension, because she growled deep in her throat. Matt didn't do a thing about it.

Russ glanced at Cleo before meeting Matt's eyes, then he crossed his arms and lifted his chin. "I think you're misunderstanding us, Matt. You've *already* used the services. Now payment must be rendered."

Matt didn't want to have to get ugly, so he would give it one last try. "Fine. Let's negotiate a price."

Russ shook his head and frowned. "That's not how this works."

Okay. He'd had enough. He was done trying to be reasonable. Gritting his teeth, he glared at Russ. "Get the hell off my property."

Cleo barked, but even so, neither Russ nor Eric moved.

With adrenaline surging, Matt reached into his waist holster, grabbed his .45, and drew down on the men. "Now." His voice was deadly calm.

Both men raised their hands like they didn't want any trouble and began backing up. "You want to do this the hard way? Fine."

Matt kept his gun pointed at them while Cleo barked in her deep, threatening voice. Once the men were out of sight, he holstered his .45 before closing and locking the door.

Shaking slightly as the adrenaline seeped away, Matt turned to his family, who all looked terrified.

CHAPTER 35

Jessica

Were those men for real? Had they really thought Matt would allow them to waltz in to their house and let them rummage through their things? She hated that he'd had to point his gun at them to make them leave, and now she was terrified that they would be back. Maybe they wouldn't. But she knew that was a false hope. Of course they'd be back. They weren't going to let Matt's defiance stand. If they did, it would topple their entire operation. Why would people go along with them taking their stuff if they found out the Bronson family had gotten medical care without joining the cooperative?

Jessica looked at her children. Brooke—who she now considered one of her own—knelt on the floor with her eyes on Cleo, then opened her arms. Cleo raced to her. Kayla had a deep V between her eyes and Dylan looked like he couldn't decide if he was scared or excited about what was happening.

"It's all my fault," Kayla said.

"No," Matt said as he went to her side. "It was bound to happen sooner or later."

"Yeah, but because I cut my finger," she held it up to emphasize her point, "it happened sooner."

Jessica joined her and Matt. "We'll deal with it, sweetheart."

A look of determination came over Kayla. "Yes." She looked at Brooke and Dylan. "All of us will. Together."

Brooke looked scared, but Dylan nodded and said, "Count me in."

That worried her more. She didn't want her children caught in the middle of this. She turned to Matt, but he was looking at the windows. Without comment, he walked to the nearest one and grabbed the security bars, shaking them in an apparent attempt to make sure they were securely latched. He checked each window on the first floor before heading to the basement stairs.

Jessica followed him. "Maybe we should barricade all the doors."

He turned to look at her, his expression saying he was glad she wasn't under the illusion that they were safe. "Yeah."

"Do you think we ought to hide some of our food? In case they, uh, they get in?"

He nodded. "That's not a bad idea."

With the kids' help, they barricaded the front door and

the sliding glass door as best they could. Next, they took all of the freeze-dried food, which were stored in buckets, and carried them out through the garage to the RV, stashing most of them under Matt and Jessica's bed and some of them in the RV's lower storage area. The last two buckets wouldn't fit anywhere, so they took out the mylar envelopes and stashed them in various places within the RV.

"Now we just have to hope no one breaks into the RV," Matt said with a frown. Jessica thought the same thing. With the RV behind their fence, hopefully that would deter thieves, but nothing was certain in this world.

When they were done, the five of them went into the house and barricaded the door to the garage, then put as many cases of canned food under their beds as they could fit, leaving a small amount in the pantry and just a few items in the basement storage room.

"Now, if they get in," Matt said with a frown, "they'll think we only have a little bit of food left."

Jessica hoped he was right, but what if they *did* get in and didn't believe that was all they had? What if they wanted to search the house?

The idea of strangers ransacking their house in search of food to steal made her furious. "Can I talk to you?" she said to Matt. "In our room?"

"Of course."

The two of them went into their bedroom. Matt turned to her with a questioning look. "What's up?"

"I was wondering if I should, you know, carry a gun."

The idea actually scared her, but what if those men got in and things got out of hand?

"I think that's a great idea. If you're comfortable with it."

Softly chuckling, she said, "I'm not super comfortable with it, but what if they get in?" Dread at the thought of those men becoming violent made her heart pound, "I need to be able to protect our children."

Matt nodded. "I agree." He went into the closet and took out a small case, setting it on their bed. He opened it, revealing a pistol. "This is a 9 millimeter."

Jessica stared at the gun. With its matte black finish and solid barrel, it looked so deadly.

"Hold it like this when you rack it," Matt said, demonstrating. "Right now it's not loaded, but you should always treat a gun like it is."

She smiled warmly. "I know. That's what Derrick said at his class."

He chuckled. "Well, he's right." He held the gun out to her.

Gingerly, she lifted it from his hand. She hefted the weight of it, then she gripped it in her left hand and tried to rack it with her right. It wasn't as easy as Matt made it look —she wasn't nearly as strong as he was. Struggling to rack it, she kept working at it until she felt comfortable. Then she sighted it, pointing it in a safe direction, before turning to Matt. "Where should I keep it?"

"Somewhere you can access it quickly but where it's out

of sight." He frowned. "You wouldn't want the bad guys to grab it first."

An image of the gun getting into the wrong hands filled her mind. "I also don't want the kids to mess with it."

Matt frowned.

Was he worried about the kids getting their hands on the gun, or, more likely, did he want them to have their own so they could help defend their home?

"Let me show you how to load it," he said.

Closely watching how he did it, then trying it herself, Jessica found herself becoming more comfortable with handling the gun. Shooting someone was something else entirely, but at least she would know how to use the gun.

"Dad!" Dylan shouted as he burst into the room, his eyes like saucers. "A bunch of men are coming down our street."

Matt dashed to the bedroom window. Jessica was right on his heels. They looked out their second story window, which overlooked the front of their house.

"Crap," Matt muttered while Jessica gasped. "I count six men."

Jessica did a quick count. "Me too."

"They're coming to our house!" Dylan squeaked out.

Terror wound its way up Jessica's throat. What were these men prepared to do?

CHAPTER 36

Matt

Matt watched the men marching across his manicured lawn and toward the front door. To his dismay, Chris was among them.

He thought of the way they'd barricaded the doors. All of a sudden it felt incredibly insufficient.

Hustling down the stairs, he felt adrenaline dumping into his bloodstream.

"What should we do?" Dylan asked.

Matt stopped where he was, then motioned toward the back door. "Help me move the barricade."

"Why?"

"I need you to get Derrick."

Panic filled Dylan's eyes. "What?"

Trying not to let Dylan's panic capture him, Matt pulled the dining room table away from the door. "Help me, son."

Dylan did. "You want me to go out there? *Alone*?"

The door was clear. Matt nodded. "You'll be fine. Hop the fence to the neighbor's yard. The men will never see you." He slid the door open. "Go! Now!"

Dylan's eyebrows bunched as he looked at his dad, then a look of resolve swept over his face. "Carl would do it." At that, Dylan raced out the door. Matt watched until Dylan had cleared the back fence, then he locked the door and rebuilt the barricade.

Smiling at Dylan's Walking Dead reference, when Jessica called his name, he spun to look at her. Her eyes were frantic. "What's going on? Where did Dylan go?"

"To get Derrick."

Jessica stared at him a moment, then her shoulders sagged. "Okay."

Pounding, loud and insistent, sounded on the front door.

Matt's heart beat just as hard. He desperately hoped Derrick was home.

"Open up," a voice demanded, "or we'll break your door down."

Cleo went into a frenzy, barking with wild abandon as she danced in front of the door.

Matt looked at Kayla and Brooke. He could tell they were trying to be brave, and as much as he appreciated their support, he didn't want them to get hurt. He motioned for them to go upstairs. "Go. Hide."

Brooke turned to flee, but Kayla stood her ground. "No. We need to stick together."

Brooke looked from Kayla to Matt to the front door, her auburn ponytail swinging. Finally, she went to Kayla's side.

"Kayla's right." Her eyes were wide with fear. "What should we do?"

He only had his .45 and the 9mm he'd given Jessica. Well, he had his rifle, but he wasn't about to hand that to either one of the girls. Not until they had experience using it. He briefly considered giving Kayla his .45, but she had no experience with it either. No, the best option was for him to keep his weapon and for her and Brooke to use something else.

The pounding sounded again with yelling following. "This is your last chance."

"Get my baseball bat," he said to Kayla, then he strode to the front door and shouted, "If you break down my door I'll blow your freaking head off!"

A brief pause, then, "You're not the only one who's armed, Matt. We've got at least six guns pointed at your house."

Alarmed, Matt tensed.

Jessica touched his arm. "Maybe we should open the door."

He looked at her sharply. "You want to let them in?"

She shook her head. "Of course not. But if we don't open the door, they'll break it down. We don't want a gunfight."

What she said made sense, and maybe it was his pride making him want to tell the men on his porch to shove it, but the thought of giving in and opening the door rankled.

"Last chance, Matt," a man yelled through the door.

Pressure built in Matt's head. He had to make a decision —possibly a life or death decision.

"I got a bat," Kayla said from beside him.

He looked at the trusting face of his sixteen-year-old daughter. A bat was no match for half a dozen guns.

Pushing a smile onto his lips, he said, "Turns out a bat won't cut it." He swallowed over the knot in his throat. "You and Brooke go upstairs. Stay up there until I tell you to come down."

The fear must have been plain on his face, because Kayla nodded, then grabbed Brooke by the hand and the two of them dashed up the stairs.

A deafening *Boom!* sounded. The door rattled in its frame.

"They're breaking it down!" Jessica screamed.

Matt remembered how easily Derrick had broken down Tony's door. Maybe it would be better to face this head on.

"Stop!" he yelled. "I'll open it." He turned to Jessica, who stood five feet behind him. He waved her to the side. "Stay out of their line of fire."

Her eyes widened. "Do you think they'll shoot?"

They'd killed Tony. Who knew what they were capable of? Not wanting to give her an answer, he waved her to the side, then pulled out his .45. Keeping it by his leg, he unlocked the deadbolt, then turned the knob.

CHAPTER 37

Matt

He opened the door slowly, his gaze going to Russ, who stood front and center. Chris was right behind him.

Cleo stood next to Matt, trying her best to shove through the door. He didn't want her to get hurt so he only opened the door about six inches

Matt focused on Russ. "You're not coming in." His tone was filled with disdain.

Russ frowned like Matt was a wayward child who needed to be taught a lesson. "You gotta cooperate, bro. We don't want this going south and I don't think you do either."

That was true. Even so, there was no way in hell he would let Russ into his house. He would shoot the man first.

Matt looked at Chris. He'd seen the way Chris had been torn about being part of the co-op, remembered that Chris had said he'd only agreed to head security as a way to feed his family. Maybe Matt should have made a side deal with Chris to help him and his family out. Then again, his own food supply wasn't unlimited.

Then he got an idea. He looked at Russ. "Chris can come in. Only Chris."

Russ stared at him. "Fine." He turned to Chris. "You know what to do."

Chris nodded. Someone from behind Chris handed him a small box.

Russ moved aside and Chris stepped forward.

Cleo's deep barking intensified. Chris looked meaningfully at Cleo before lifting his gaze to Matt.

Matt held Cleo's collar. "It's all right, girl." She settled down and Matt stepped back enough to allow Chris to enter. The moment Chris cleared the threshold, Matt closed and locked the door.

"What happens now?" Matt asked, glad Russ had agreed to let Chris come in alone. He didn't want anyone coming in, but he could at least stomach letting Chris in.

Chris grimaced. "Now you show me your food supply and I take some of it."

Even though Matt and his family had hidden the vast majority of their food, the idea that an outsider could force his way in, rummage through their personal items, then take what he wanted ripped a deep streak of resentment right through him. But what could he do? Six armed men were at his house, and by all appearances they would take what they wanted by force. Were a few cans of green beans worth dying over?

Trying not to grit his teeth, Matt said, "You can look in the pantry."

With an expression of discomfort, Chris nodded. "Show me where that is."

Matt felt himself tensing up.

"This way," Jessica said, saving him from having to say something he might regret.

Matt watched Jessica lead the way into the kitchen. He followed Chris, watching with clenched fists as Chris carefully looked over what they had. Chris took out several cans of food, including chili and vegetables, placing them in the box which he'd set on the counter. He added a packet of crackers to the pile, then turned to them with a tight smile, "Do you have any food in your basement?"

Pressure was building in Matt's head. He thought he might explode. This time he couldn't stop his teeth from clenching as he spoke. "You've taken enough."

Shaking his head, Chris sighed. "The rule is to take twenty percent of all food stores."

Blood rushed to Matt's face. "Twenty percent!? Do you want to take one of my kids for slave labor too?"

Chris's face reddened as his jaw tightened. "Just show me your basement."

More grateful than ever that they'd hidden most of their food, he had to slowly breathe in and out, in and out.

Jessica placed her hand on Matt's arm. "I'll show him. You stay here."

Filled with rage, Matt didn't respond.

Five minutes later Chris and Jessica emerged from the

basement. Chris held half a dozen cans of food. He went to the kitchen counter and set them in the box, then he picked up the box and turned to Matt. "I'm sorry about this." A look of indecision came over him. "I'm not going to ask if you have food anywhere else."

Matt gazed at him. Did Chris suspect they had more and he was purposefully ignoring that? Feeling his rage dissipating a hair, Matt didn't reply. Instead, he walked to the front door. Chris took the hint and followed. Matt opened the door. Chris went out and handed the box to Russ, who looked over the goods inside. When a smug grin formed on Russ's lips, Matt's rage reignited and it took all of his self-control not to wipe the expression right off of Russ's face.

"Thank you for your donation," Russ said with a smirk.

Livid, Matt's nostrils flared. "I assume our family will be covered by your security and medical services now."

Russ made a scoffing sound. "'Fraid not, Matthew. This just covers payment for Dr. Larsen's services."

He couldn't believe the audacity of these people. First, they demanded that Matt pay *them* for services that should have been handled between Matt and Dr. Larsen, then they threatened to break his door down and made it clear they would shoot him, and when he let them in, they took whatever they wanted. And now they said the "payment" only covered the stitches Dr. Larsen gave Kayla and nothing else?

Blood boiling, rage erupting, Matt couldn't take it any longer. He'd had enough. He stepped onto the porch and lunged for the box of food. Russ yanked it away.

"What do you think you're doing?" Russ asked.

Matt stood inches from him. "Taking back what's mine."

Russ shook his head. "Nope. This is no longer yours. It now belongs to the cooperative."

Feeling like his head was about to blast right off of his shoulders, Matt didn't even think before he drew his .45, pointing it in Russ's face. "Wrong. Now, set it down and walk away."

Russ just laughed. That's when Matt realized that the other five men were pointing their guns at him.

"Looks like you're outgunned, Matthew."

"Think again," a deep voice said from behind the men arrayed on Matt's porch.

All eyes swiveled in the direction of the voice, including Matt's. A thrill of relief swept over him as a grin curved his lips.

Derrick, Jeff, Emily, and Dylan stood behind the men, all of them pointing guns at the intruders. Derrick and Jeff held two guns each, one in each hand. With Matt's gun pointed at Russ, that was a total of seven guns pointed at the men from the cooperative.

Russ looked at Matt, slight panic filling his eyes. With the box held in his hands, he was the only person not armed.

"Tell your men to drop their weapons," Matt said calmly, although his fury was still burning bright.

Russ's eyes widened. "You're taking our guns?"

Matt grinned. This was so sweet. "Looks that way."

Using his chin, he gestured to the box of food. "Put that down too."

Russ's face turned bright red, but he loudly said over his shoulder, "You heard the man."

The five men set their guns down.

"Step back," Derrick said, giving the men room to walk past him.

Russ looked at Matt, muttering, "You're gonna regret this."

Matt had no doubt that this was the start of a war, but it was too late to turn back now. They had to take a stand.

Not responding to Russ's threat, Matt chin-gestured to the box of food. "Put it down."

A muscle worked in Russ's jaw, but he set the box down.

"Arms up," Matt said.

Russ complied.

Keeping his gun fixed on Russ, Matt took Russ's gun out of his waistband. "Join your buddies."

Russ glared at Matt. "You and your family won't be in this neighborhood for long." Then he turned and stormed away.

Matt watched the six men make their way across the grass and down the sidewalk. Once they were out of sight, Matt breathed a sigh of relief, but it was a short breath because he knew this was only the beginning of their troubles.

CHAPTER 38

Jessica

Jessica's heart was still pounding. What if Derrick and the others hadn't shown up when they had? What if a gunfight had ensued? Dylan would have been in the middle of it.

Torn between gratitude to Derrick and his friends for showing up just in time and anger that Derrick had put a gun in Dylan's hands, Jessica stood behind Matt and listened as Matt thanked Derrick and his friends for coming. They gathered the guns the men had left, then Matt introduced Jessica to Derrick's friends.

"Hi," Jessica said, stepping back to allow everyone to come inside. As Dylan walked past her wearing a huge grin, she narrowed her eyes at him.

"Hi, Mom," he said.

"Give that gun back to Derrick," she said in reply.

"Then go get the girls and let them know it's safe to come down."

Disappointment washed over his face, but he gave Derrick the gun he'd been holding, then went up the stairs.

Jessica went into the family room where the group was assembling. Cleo lay on the floor at Matt's feet. The men set the guns on the coffee table.

"These will definitely help," Matt said, then he looked at Derrick and Jeff. "How do you want to divide them up?"

"How many do you need?" Derrick asked.

Matt glanced at Jessica before turning back to Derrick. "At least three."

"Take four," Derrick said as he pushed them toward Matt. "Jeff and I will take the other two."

Not sure if she liked the idea of more guns in the house, Jessica was also torn. If they'd had more guns initially—one for each person in their family—they wouldn't have been so outnumbered by the men of the co-op. Of course, she and the kids had zero experience firing guns whereas the men of the co-op surely had experience. Still, having extra firearms would be a good start.

"Thank you," she said to Derrick as she sat beside Matt. "That will help."

Matt looked at her in surprise. She slipped her hand into his. They had to be on the same page. If they weren't a team, their entire family would suffer.

Dylan and the girls joined them.

"What happened, Mom?" Kayla asked.

She and Matt recounted the frightening events. Kayla and Brooke listened with shocked faces.

"What do you think those guys will do now?" Kayla asked.

Jessica wondered the same thing.

Derrick shook his head. "No doubt they'll retaliate. And since they know how much food you have, you can bet your last can of chili that they want every bit of it."

That wasn't what Jessica wanted to hear, although he was only confirming what she already knew. She thought about Russ's parting words. "They said we won't be in the neighborhood for long."

Matt gently squeezed her hand. "They don't get to decide who belongs here."

That may have been true, but in the world they lived in now, a group like the co-op's could make it impossible for their family to stay.

"We have to be ready for anything," Jeff said.

"You'll help us?" Jessica asked, thrilled to know they wouldn't be alone.

Emily nodded with a smile.

Jeff chuckled. "We're the ones who flanked them. We're in it just as much as you are now."

Matt turned to Derrick. "Any ideas on what we should do to prepare?"

Everyone was quiet as they considered options, all the while Jessica's heart raced. The men of the co-op had to be furious over what had happened. No doubt they would be thrilled if the Bronson family left—as well as Derrick and Jeff and Emily.

"I have a plan," Derrick said. Everyone looked to him. "Are the houses on either side of yours occupied?"

Matt looked at Jessica. She shrugged. "I'm not sure, but I doubt it. I, uh, I haven't seen anyone around for over a week."

"What about the houses across the street?"

"Same thing there," Matt said.

Nodding, Derrick said, "Perfect. We'll scope out the surrounding houses and choose the ones with the best vantage point of your house. Then," he looked at Matt and Jessica, "you'll take your family and temporarily move into a neighbor's house."

Though she wanted to protest, she decided to hear him out.

"I'll stay in a different house," he continued, "and Jeff and Emily will stay in another. That way you'll be out of the target house and we'll all be in a good position when they strike. That's when we'll strike first."

She liked it. Go on offense.

Then she frowned. She couldn't believe what she was thinking. The men they were planning on going on offense against were people who were in her neighborhood. Now they were enemies? Then she considered history. During the Civil War many neighbors had joined ranks, but others had fought against each other.

Subtly shaking her head, she focused on the conversation.

"We should move anything of value," Matt said, "like food and water, out of this house. There's no telling what they'll do to our house."

What did he mean? Did he think those men would destroy her house? Angered and saddened all at the same time, she didn't know what to say.

"What about the RV?" Dylan, who'd been taking it all in, asked. "Should we move that? It's pretty valuable."

"Absolutely," Matt said with a smile.

"I know a safe place you can store it," Derrick said. "There's an older house at the end of my street with a barn in the back. One of those houses that was here way before they built our neighborhood. Unfortunately, the man who owns the place didn't make it. But that means it's up for grabs. I, uh, I checked it out a few days ago and there's some old junk in the barn, but there's enough room for your rig."

Matt nodded. "Great idea."

Derrick turned to Jeff and Emily. "Our houses could be targets as well. We ought to gather our food and supplies and stash them in the barn too."

"Works for me," Jeff said.

Knowing they were all in this together gave Jessica a feeling of being on a team—a very experienced team.

Derrick stood. "Let's check out the houses next door. We need to get ready asap."

CHAPTER 39

Matt

Grateful they weren't in this alone, Matt stood as well, then he turned to Jessica and the kids. "Gather all the food in the house, as well as the things we got from Costco and Amazon last week, and put them in the RV. Then we'll have everything in one place."

"What about our seedlings?" Kayla asked.

Matt pictured the dozens of trays of seedlings they'd planted. Where would they put them? The RV had limited space. Food had to take priority. "I'm sorry, Kayla. We're going to have to leave them."

Her face fell.

Not wanting to remove all hope, he said, "When this thing with the co-op is resolved, we'll come back and they'll still be here."

Her face tightened, then she shook her head before looking away. "Whatever."

Jessica put her arm around Kayla. "We can get more seeds." She threw a small smile at Matt before leading Kayla, Brooke, and Dylan toward the kitchen.

Matt turned to Jeff and Derrick. "Do you think it's wise to put everything in one place? I mean, what if Russ, Eric, and the rest steal it from the barn while we're here?"

"Unless they see us moving it, they won't have a clue that it's there." Derrick paused. "What about having your kids stay in the barn with a walkie talkie? They can keep an eye on things and if there's a problem they can let us know. We'd be there within a minute."

Matt looked toward Jessica, who was listening from the kitchen. "What do you think?"

Grimacing, she said, "I don't know. Seems risky."

Derrick looked her way. "There are plenty of places to hide in that barn if they need to stay out of sight. Besides, they'd be safer there than here where I expect the fight to take place."

Jessica looked at Matt. He nodded. Derrick made sense.

"Okay," she said, though her tone held reluctance. "But the safety of the kids comes first."

"You could stay there with them," Matt said. Having her far away from the fight would be a bonus.

She nodded. "True." Then she paused. "Let me think about it."

Good enough.

"Let's go," Derrick said.

With that, Matt, Derrick, Jeff, and Emily masked and gloved up and walked out of the house.

"Matt," Derrick said, "you're with me. Jeff and Emily, you search those houses." He pointed to the house on the north side of Matt's as well as two houses across the street.

Jeff and Emily headed one way while Matt and Derrick headed the other.

They went to the neighboring house on the south side. A red X was painted on the door.

Great. Another body.

Derrick motioned to the door in a *You do the honors* motion. Matt frowned, but he put his hand on the knob and turned. To his surprise, it was unlocked and the door swung inward. The stench was worse than it had been at Tony's. Trying to control his gag reflex, he turned to Derrick. "I don't know if any of us can stay in these houses if they smell like this."

Derrick slowly shook his head as if to say *We'll do what we have to do.*

Right.

Matt stepped inside.

Derrick pointed to the kitchen. Matt followed him, and when Derrick opened the pantry and Matt saw that the shelves were bare, he looked at Derrick in mild surprise.

"The co-op's been here," Derrick said.

There was no way to know for sure if that was who had cleaned the place out, but it seemed like the logical answer.

They quickly went through the rest of the house before heading to the house across the street from Matt's. That house didn't have a red X on the door, which gave Matt hope that it wouldn't smell like death.

The front door was locked.

"I don't want to kick the door in," Derrick said. "Might make it obvious we're inside. Let's go around back instead."

They found the sliding glass door unlocked. After making sure the house was empty—no bodies or stink of death this time—they checked the pantry. No surprise. It was empty.

"This house will work," Derrick said.

They checked the house next to it, which was a little farther from Matt's house. Two dead bodies and nothing in the pantry.

They went back to Matt's house where they met up with Jeff and Emily. Derrick reported on what they'd found, then they listened to Jeff and Emily's report.

"House to the north is clear," Jeff said. "The house across the street had one body. The location was stellar though, so we dragged the body out back. The house north of that was clear."

Matt's eyebrows shot up at the mention of dragging out a body. When he saw that Derrick wasn't bothered by the notion, he forced himself to relax.

"Okay," Derrick said, looking at each of them. "We have a selection of houses." Then he turned to Jeff. "Did you happen to check for food?"

"Of course. And you were right. Completely empty."

"Uh-huh," Derrick said with a scowl and a shake of his head.

Jessica and the kids joined them. “We loaded all the supplies into the RV.”

“Excellent,” Matt said. He gazed at her a moment. “Have you made a decision? About the kids staying in the barn?”

She nodded.

“We’ll do it,” Dylan said with complete confidence.

Matt looked at Brooke and Kayla. They nodded too.

“Can we keep Cleo with us?” Brooke asked.

That was a good idea. She would protect them. “Of course.”

A smile of relief curved Brooke’s lips.

Matt looked at Jessica. “What about you? Will you stay in the barn with the kids?”

Jessica looked at Emily. “How comfortable are you with guns?”

Emily laughed. “I’m with this guy,” she jabbed a thumb in Jeff’s direction. “In other words, very comfortable.” She smiled. “We target shoot all the time and I’ve been hunting with him a fair number of times.”

Jessica bit her lip. “Would you be willing to go with me and the kids to the barn? I, uh, I wouldn’t mind having someone who has experience shooting a gun with us.”

Emily looked at Jeff, who said, “It’s up to you, babe.”

Frowning, Emily said, “But then it will just be the three of you against how many?”

Jeff chuckled. “We can handle it.” He paused. “Go with Jessica.”

Matt would feel better knowing someone with more experience was with Jess and the kids.

"All right," Emily said, "but we'll keep in contact and I can come if you need me."

Once that was settled, Matt and Jessica worked together to hitch the RV to his truck. Then Jessica, the kids, and Cleo loaded into the truck and they followed Derrick to the barn, doing their best to make sure no one had followed them.

When they reached the barn, Matt backed right in. No reason to leave the RV in sight any longer than necessary. There were two man-doors, one in the back and one in the front. And just as Derrick had said, there was plenty of room for his rig. And lots of good places to hide if necessary.

Once Jessica and the kids and Cleo were situated, Matt left the RV hitched to his truck and walked with Derrick to his place to help him gather the supplies he wanted to stash in the barn. He put several containers of gas in the back of his truck. By the time they got back to the barn in Derrick's truck—which they parked just outside the doors—Jeff and Emily had arrived with their supplies. They had a small utility trailer behind Jeff's truck, which they parked in the barn.

Both Derrick and Jeff had their own walkie talkies. They put theirs and Matt's on the same channel, which gave them enough walkies for each adult in the group and one for the kids to share.

"It'll be dark soon," Jeff said to the group. "I'm gonna

head over to the blue house across the street from Matt's place. I'll take a walkie and let you know if I see anything."

"Sounds good," Derrick said. "We'll be along soon."

Jeff gave Emily a kiss, then he trotted out of the barn.

CHAPTER 40

Matt

Ten minutes after Jeff left the barn, the walkies squawked. "COMM check."

"It's Jeff," Derrick said. He pressed a button and held his walkie to his mouth. "Copy."

"In position."

"Roger that." Wearing his game face, Derrick looked at Matt. "We leave in twenty."

Matt felt out of his league, but at least Jeff and Derrick knew what they were doing because he was sure things were going to get rough. All the more reason for Jess and the kids to be here, far, far away from the action.

Twenty minutes later, heavily armed, he and Derrick got in Derrick's truck. Derrick parked one street over from Matt's house. They went the rest of the way on foot. When they arrived at the blue house, they checked in with Jeff.

"No sign of anyone," Jeff said with barely a glance

before his gaze went back to the window that overlooked Matt's house.

Derrick nodded. "It's getting dark. If I were in charge I'd hit when it's full dark." His jaw tightened. "And you know they would've put Chris in charge."

"Yeah," Jeff said.

"What do you want me to do?" Matt asked.

Pointing to the house on the north side of Matt's house, Derrick said, "Stake out your house from the second story of that house. If you see anyone, give us two squawks on the walkie like this." He demonstrated. "It's an open line, and although we're using a random channel, there's still a possibility that the wrong person will join our party line. Then squawk once before squawking how many people you see."

They discussed other signals and code words they would use. Matt just hoped he would remember everything. He nodded. "Got it."

"I'll be in the house to the south of this one," Derrick said.

At that, they split up. Matt made his way to the house next door to his, staying close to the tree line. When he reached the front porch, it occurred to him that someone from the co-op could already be inside. What if they'd come early to stake things out as well?

Heart slamming against his ribs, he turned the knob and pushed the door slowly open. When nothing happened, he stepped inside, closing the door behind him. His eyes had already adjusted to the dim light outside, but it was much darker in the house.

Pausing a moment with his eyes closed, listening, he reminded himself that he was not alone in this. That Derrick and Jeff were fully on board, that they had combat experience, and that the men of the co-op didn't know that Matt and his family had left their house.

Not a sound. He opened his eyes and could make out the furniture and the shape of the room. Much better.

Feeling more confident, he cleared the first floor using his .45 the way Derrick had shown him when they'd checked the other houses earlier. With his .45 in his hand and his rifle strapped to his back, he climbed the stairs to the second floor. After quickly clearing that floor, he went to the bedrooms to find which one had the best vantage point. The one in the back had a clear view of his backyard. He opened the window and removed the screen, then slid the window closed. Getting comfortable, he parked himself in front of the window, letting his eyes sweep every inch of his property that was within view.

As he waited and watched, he wondered if the men from the co-op would strike tonight or wait for another night when Matt and his family would be relaxed and unprepared. As the minutes ticked by he began to think their plan was the latter.

Until he saw two men appear at his backyard neighbor's fence.

Startled, he stared at them for a full second before grabbing the walkie and doing two short squawks. He followed it up with one squawk, a pause, then two more squawks. The men hopped the fence, landing in Matt's backyard. Two more men appeared at the fence line, climbing the fence to join their buddies. Matt squawked once, then two more times. Would Derrick know what he meant?

Straining to see if he recognized any of the four, when his walkie squawked once, then twice, he jerked. That's when he saw a pair of men coming into the backyard through the gate. Derrick or Jeff had seen them. Good.

His eyes were riveted on the action below. Five of the men were holding things in their hands, but from this distance and in the dark, he couldn't tell what they were holding. Only one man had empty hands. Matt couldn't tell who it was, but he was the only one wearing a ball cap.

A sudden bright flame nearly blinded him. Then another and another. Then two more.

Before he had a chance to react, every man but the one in the ball cap were throwing Molotov cocktails at the windows of his house. Glass shattered, but with the security bars on the inside, the flaming bottles fell back to the ground outside.

Panicked that they were going to burn his house down, Matt completely forgot the protocol they'd set up. Instead, pressing the Talk button, he said, "They're trying to set my house on fire!"

What if he and his family had been inside? Would those men care? Or were they trying to draw them out so they could shoot them?

Fury, powerful and black, surged through him. These

men were ruthless. First trying to steal their food, and now trying to burn them out. He had to do something, had to stop them.

He set the walkie on the ground, then after sliding the window open, he used his rifle to sight in on one of the men, sliding his finger to the trigger. Then it hit him. He would be killing in cold blood. Was he really prepared to take that step?

Derrick must have known the way Matt would react—maybe the way he'd seen him nearly blow Charlie's head off the week before had clued him in—because the walkie squawked and one word came across. "Hold."

CHAPTER 41

Matt

Matt's gaze shot to the walkie as his finger slid away from the trigger. Derrick was right. He needed to reign in his emotions and focus on what was happening.

The Molotov cocktails had been a failure. His house didn't appear to be on fire.

Staring at the men, Matt watched as they seemed to wait in ambush for Matt and his family to come running out. When no one did, the men went into a loose huddle. What would their next move be? Had they figured out that Matt and his family weren't inside?

Matt felt a light tap on his shoulder while at the same time he heard Derrick's voice beside him, "It's me."

Heart thumping at Derrick's unexpected appearance—could anyone else have snuck up on him?—Matt turned to Derrick with a frown before both men looked out the window. Then, to Matt's stunned surprise, one of the men broke off from the group, pulled out a gun, and blasted the sliding glass door to bits. The men rushed inside. Except the man in the ball cap. Was he their lookout?

Matt turned to Derrick. "Should we take him out?"

Derrick stared at Matt. "Not yet." Then he smiled. "Won't they be surprised when there's nothing worth taking?"

Though that may have been true, it still made Matt's blood boil to think of those men ransacking his home. "We should go in there."

Derrick's eyebrows rose. "And do what? Get into a gunfight? Over what?" He shook his head. "I only risk my life when something of value is at stake."

But it was his house. Then he pictured his family. Was keeping those men out worth dying over? No.

Frustration building, he stared at the house, waiting to see what would happen next.

It didn't take long.

Five minutes later the men poured out of the broken sliding glass door. Moments after that, smoke followed. They'd set the house on fire from the inside. Then the five men who'd gone in the house pulled out their guns and began shooting out all the windows.

Matt didn't care what Derrick said, these men had to be stopped. They'd killed Tony and now they'd set his house on fire. Did they think Matt and his family were asleep upstairs? Were they trying to kill them?

Without looking to Derrick for approval, Matt rested the

rifle barrel on the frame of the open window and sighted in on one of the men shooting at his house. Expecting Derrick to stop him, when instead Derrick pointed his gun at the men and said, "I've got the one on the far right," Matt slid his gaze to Derrick in surprise before saying, "Far left."

Half a second later, the blast of Derrick's gun filled Matt's ears. The man on the far right dropped and the other five men looked around in confusion, searching for where the blast had come from. Soon they would know exactly where to aim their guns. There was no time to hesitate. Their position had been revealed. Forcing all unnecessary thoughts away, Matt turned his focus to aiming true, sighting in on the man on the far left. He pulled the trigger. To his stunned surprise, the man fell.

Four men were left, but just as they found the window where Matt and Derrick knelt and raised their guns to fire, the man in the ball cap turned his gun on the man beside him and shot him dead. Then he shot the next man, who fell to the ground. The last man dropped at the same time. Matt's gaze jerked to the side of his yard where he saw Jeff standing, pointing a gun at the man who'd fallen last. Jeff shifted his gun to the man in the ball cap and yelled, "Drop your weapon and get on the ground." The man did it immediately.

Overwhelmed by all that had just happened, Matt took a moment to catch his breath. He would have to take time to mentally process it later.

"Let's go," Derrick said.

At that, Matt and Derrick leapt up and cautiously made

their way down the stairs and toward Matt's backyard, careful to make sure no other men were hiding in wait. They joined Jeff in Matt's backyard.

Matt's eyes went to the five men who were down. Not one of them moved. Among them were Russ and Eric. Were they all dead? Sickened by the thought that he was responsible for any of their deaths, when the smell of smoke filled his nostrils and he turned to see his house in flames and saw all the windows shattered by the men's' bullets, any sorrow he'd begun to feel was wiped away. These men hadn't had to do this. They hadn't had to get in the middle of Matt and Dr. Larsen's interaction at all. They'd inserted themselves where they didn't need to be, prepared to take twenty percent of the Bronson family's food. For themselves. And when that hadn't worked, they'd come after Matt and his family, prepared to kill them.

Rage at their audacity blasted through him. Then he looked at the man who was face down on the ground. It was the man in the ball cap. Narrowing his eyes, Matt recognized him in the dim moonlight. It was Chris. He was the one man who hadn't thrown a Molotov cocktail at Matt's house, the one man who hadn't gone inside to set his house on fire, the one man who hadn't shot at his house. The man who had killed the others to keep them from shooting at Matt and Derrick.

Jeff holstered his weapon and gestured to Chris with his chin. "What do you want to do with him?"

"Let him go," Derrick said. "He's not the bad guy here."

"He took out two of them," Matt said, pointing to the dead men on the grass.

"I know," Jeff said. "I saw him do it. That's when I moved in."

Chris got to his feet, his face showing clear remorse. "I wanted to warn you they were coming," he said to Matt, "but I didn't get the chance." He sighed. "I tried to talk them out of setting your house on fire but Russ was livid that you'd taken his guns." A small smirk tugged up one side of Chris's mouth. "Nice move, by the way."

Remembering the way Chris had taken twenty percent of the food he'd found, Matt felt his anger rekindle. "You were part of them."

Chris's chin lowered toward his chest, then he looked at Matt, his eyes bracketed with anxiety and fear. "I did it for my family."

Picturing Chris's wife and small children, Matt couldn't fault him for agreeing to join the cooperative. And the fact that he'd actually killed two of the men, which quite literally could have saved Matt and Derrick's lives… Matt wasn't going to fault him. Besides, he remembered Chris purposely not looking through his house for hidden food.

"Look," Chris said, "we can work this out later, but you need to know," he looked at Derrick and Jeff, "they were sending other men to hit your houses. I'm pretty sure they knew I wasn't on board with their plans so they didn't tell me everything. You might want to check on your places."

"We'll take my truck," Derrick said. "I'll drop Jeff and

Chris's off near Jeff's house, then Matt and I will go to mine."

Matt looked at his house where the flames were growing ever brighter. "What about my house?"

"I'm sorry," Derrick said. "There's nothing we can do about it."

Matt knew he was right. "Let's make sure the same thing doesn't happen to your or Jeff's house."

"Thanks," he said.

The four of them took off at a run to the next street where Derrick had parked his truck.

CHAPTER 42

Jessica

What was happening at her house? Sitting on the tailgate of Matt's truck in the barn lit only by the moonlight trickling through a high window, Jessica gripped the walkie in her hand, frantic with worry. She'd heard Matt say that someone was trying to burn their house down. The thought made her sick. Especially when she considered what would have happened if they hadn't left. What was wrong with those men? Had hunger made them lose their minds completely?

Then she'd heard Derrick say "Hold." Why? Had something else happened? Listening to events unfold without knowing what was going on was torture. She was desperate to get an update, but she knew radio silence was critical. She looked at Emily, who seemed completely calm. Then again, it wasn't *her* house that was being threatened. She looked at her children, who seemed as freaked out as she was.

"What do you think's happening?" she asked Emily.

The tall brunette shook her head. "Not sure, but they said they were going to watch your house from neighboring houses, so I'm sure they're perfectly safe."

"Until they attack those men," Dylan said with a scowl. "We should help them. Three against who knows how many. It's not a fair fight."

Emily tilted her head. "They can handle it. We'd just get in the way."

Glad that Emily had spoken up, Jessica nodded. "I agree. We stay here as planned."

Dylan scowled harder, then he looked away.

They sat there in the dimly lit space, waiting, waiting, waiting. It was killing her. She had to get out. With a glance at Dylan, who was still sulking as he sat on a stack of boxes, she jumped off the tailgate and walked over to him. "Let's go for a walk."

He looked at her with a frown. "What for?"

She gave him her best *Do what I say* look. "Come on."

With a huff of annoyance, he stood and walked with her to the man-door at the front of the barn. He opened it and stepped through. She followed. It was lighter outside, though with only a sliver of a moon, not all that bright.

She inhaled the fresh air and tilted her head back with her eyes closed. "Mmm. It's nice out here isn't it?"

"Yeah," Dylan said. "I guess so."

She turned to look at him. "I appreciate your enthusiasm

in wanting to help Dad, but we have to think things through. If we show up, it will throw off their plans. They'd have to adjust for us and most likely protect us. That would put everyone in danger."

His scowl was back. "I know." Then he looked at her with wide eyes. "But I want to help! I want to protect our family too!"

She drew him into her arms. "I know you do, sweetheart, and I love you for it. But there are times we need to let those with more experience take the lead and listen to what they say." She pulled away and tried to smile, but as she considered her next words, it was impossible. "You'll have your chance."

A noise caught Jessica's attention. She looked in the direction of the sound, which was toward the houses in the neighborhood. Two men were running away from a house. Then she heard a loud *whoosh!* Was it coming from Derrick's house?

"What was that?" Dylan whispered.

Jessica walked away from the barn to get a better look, but she didn't see where the men had gone. Her eyes slid to the walkie at her hip. She had no idea what was going on at her house, but she felt like she should tell the men that something was happening here.

With slight hesitation, she lifted the walkie from her hip, then pressed the Talk button. "Something's happening on your street." She knew they would know where she meant.

A bright flame lit the night sky. She pressed the Talk

button again. "Fire!" She hooked the walkie onto her hip then turned to Dylan. "Let's go."

With Dylan by her side, they ran toward the barn. Cleo was barking frantically from inside. What was happening? What had gotten Cleo so upset?

"We need to be quiet," she said to Dylan as she turned the volume on the walkie down before creeping toward the man-door.

He nodded.

She opened the door a few inches, then held back a gasp. Two men were inside. They were in the process of tying up Kayla and Emily. Cleo was restrained by her leash, but she was barking and growling. Brooke was nowhere in sight. Where was she? Had the men done something to her? Terror at the thought skated over Jessica's skin. The poor girl had been through enough.

Quietly closing the door, Jessica stepped back, then lifted the walkie to tell the men what was going on. A hand clamped over her mouth while an arm wrapped tightly around her arms, pinning them to her side. The walkie fell from her hand. Terrified, she fought back, twisting and kicking, but it did no good.

"Stop fighting or we shoot the boy."

Eyes going wide, Jessica froze. They had a gun on Dylan? How many men were there? Were they the same men she'd seen running from Derrick's house, or other men completely?

The man turned Jessica so she could see he was telling the truth. Another man held a gun to Dylan's head. Dylan looked on the verge of tears, all of his earlier bravado gone.

"Are you gonna behave?" the man said in her ear.

Wanting nothing more than to draw her gun and shoot him dead, she nodded.

"Good." He released her mouth and arms. "I'll take this." She felt him taking the gun out of the waistband of her jeans. He pointed her gun at her, then gestured to the man-door. "Go inside."

Hoping and praying that Matt and the others wouldn't be too distracted by the fire...that's when she knew. The men of the co-op had known all along that all of their goods were inside this barn. They must have seen them moving their RV as well as Jeff parking his utility trailer inside. Had they set the fires to distract the fighters in their group so they could take everything of value when they were at their most vulnerable?

Furious at the thought, she spun around and shoved the man behind her with all her might. He was taken off guard and fell back a step, but he held on to the gun.

"What the...?" he asked as he glared at her. He stepped forward and gripped her upper arm until she cried out in pain.

"Let my mom go!" Dylan shouted.

"Shut up," the man with the gun on Dylan growled.

"Everyone in the barn," the first man said.

Still fuming, Jessica did as instructed, opening the door and stepping inside. The two men already in the barn strode toward them, one of them dragging Jessica near Emily and

Kayla, zip-tying her hands in front of her. Dylan joined her a moment later with his hands tied as well.

"Are you okay?" she asked the three of them.

They nodded.

"They took the walkie talkies," Emily said with a grimace.

Now there was no way to call for help.

A man wearing a blue shirt came over to Jessica and knelt in front of her. "Where are the keys to the trucks?"

She looked at the two trucks in the barn—one hitched to the RV, the other to the utility trailer. "I don't know."

He scowled at her. "You wouldn't lie to me, would you?"

Of course she would. She shook her head. "No."

"Good. Because I'd hate to have to shoot one of these kids to get you to tell me the truth."

That got her attention. "I *am* telling you the truth. I don't know where the keys are." In all reality, Matt and Jeff had the keys.

The man shook his head then went to talk to the other three men.

"I'm scared, Mom," Kayla whispered.

"It'll be okay," she whispered back, although she knew no such thing. Glancing at the men to make sure they weren't listening, she leaned toward the Kayla. "Where's Brooke?"

Kayla shook her head. "I don't know. She went out the back door to go to the bathroom right after you left."

That could be good news or bad. If the men hadn't seen

her, then it was good news. But if they had and hadn't brought her inside, that could only mean she was hurt or worse.

She couldn't let herself think of that just then.

"What do they want?" Kayla asked.

"I think they want our supplies."

"Stop talking!" Blue Shirt said. He seemed to be the one in charge.

Ignoring his command, Jessica asked, "What do you want?"

He knelt in front of her and enunciated his words like she was an idiot. "I. Want. The. Keys."

If it came to their lives or their things, of course she would do what she could to get the keys for him. Otherwise, she would be damned if she would give him any of their stuff. If what Matt had said on the walkie was true and the group these men were with was burning their house down, then the RV and what was in it was all they had in the world.

She stared at the man in defiance. "I. Don't. Have. Them."

Fury broadcast from his eyes. He reached out and slapped her across the face. Hard.

Her head snapped back and she cried out in shock and pain. At the look in his eyes, she knew things were only going to get worse.

CHAPTER 43

Matt

"We're too late," Derrick said as the men climbed out of his truck in front of his house.

The moment Jessica had called them over the walkie to report something happening at Derrick's house, Matt, Jeff, Derrick, and Chris had raced over there. When Jessica's message had reached them, they'd just gotten to Jeff's house, which was already engulfed in flames.

Now, as they watched smoke and flames billowing out of Derrick's front window, all Matt could think about was his family. Were they okay? When he'd tried to reach Jessica, she hadn't responded.

He grabbed his walkie again and pressed the Talk button. "Jess, are you there?" He waited a moment. "Jess? If you can hear me, please answer."

"Mr. Bronson!" Brooke yelled as she ran up to them, her eyes wild with panic.

"Brooke?" Matt asked. "What are you doing here? What's wrong?" Seeing her there when she was supposed to be in the barn with his family sent alarm bells ringing in his head. "Where is everyone? Are they okay?"

Shaking her head from side to side she said, "No. Some men broke in and took them hostage."

"Hostage?" He looked at Chris as if he should know about this, but he shook his head like he was clueless. Matt turned to Brooke. "How did you get away?"

"I left to go to the bathroom. When I was on my way back I saw some men sneaking up to the barn. I didn't want to call you on the walkie talkie because I was afraid they would hear too."

"How many?" Derrick asked.

"Two for sure. Maybe more."

No wonder Jess wasn't answering on her walkie. She couldn't. Matt set his jaw. "I'm going."

Derrick grabbed his arm. "Hang on. We can't go in there without a plan."

This time it wasn't his house he was trying to protect, it was his family. A million times more valuable. He knew Derrick was right, but he wasn't willing to wait long. Every second counted. Matt turned to Chris. "What do they want? Revenge?"

Chris shook his head. "I don't know. I didn't even know they were going to the barn. Why's your family in there anyway?"

"To stay away from the fight, for one thing," Matt said. "We also moved some supplies in there." Had he said too much? Could Chris be trusted?

Slowly nodding, Chris said, "I know a man was assigned to keep an eye on your house after the, uh, altercation earlier. He must have seen you taking your stuff there."

Spotting a thirty-three foot RV wouldn't be difficult. Of course they'd seen them moving it. "Are you saying they're after our supplies?"

"Most likely."

He would trade his food for his family in a heartbeat, but he wasn't sure the men of the co-op would be that easy to work with. Not after what had happened earlier. But if the men knew their leaders, Eric and Russ, were dead, would that change their minds?

Matt was quiet a moment, his mind spinning. "I can give myself in trade as a hostage."

All eyes shifted to him.

He grimaced. "Okay. I have a plan, but I don't know if you guys are going to like it."

CHAPTER 44

Jessica

Jessica's mind raced and her heart slammed against her ribs as she catalogued how dire their situation was. She and her children and Emily were tied up, held captive by four men who wanted to take what they had. Brooke was missing—maybe hurt, maybe dead. Matt and Derrick and Jeff had no idea what was happening. Her house might be on fire. Derrick's house was most certainly on fire.

Then she thought about the message she'd managed to get out. The one that told the men that something was happening in Derrick's neighborhood, that there was a fire. Derrick's house was close. Surely Matt and the other two men would come check on them in the barn. Maybe there was hope after all.

Heart settling, spirit calming, Jessica briefly closed her eyes, and when she looked at her children and reminded herself that they were all right, her despair lessened. Everything would be okay. Matt and the others would come to check on them, they would see what was happening, and they would save them.

As she imagined how it would play out, hope surged inside her.

A loud knock sounded at the rear barn door. One of the men went to it, his gun drawn.

Panicked that it was Matt, Jessica nearly called out that he was in danger. Then it occurred to her that he would have no reason to knock. If it wasn't Matt, who could it be?

"It's Chris," a voice called out.

Jessica's eyes widened. Chris was the man who'd come to their house earlier that day to take their food. Matt had told her Chris was the head of security for the neighborhood cooperative. What was he doing there? Were more men from the cooperative on their way?

The man who'd slapped Jessica pulled the door open. She couldn't see what was happening outside the door—it was too dark—but she saw the man grin like he'd just been handed the prize he'd been waiting for.

As a sense of unease swept over her, Jessica kept her gaze riveted to the door. Matt stepped through, his face downcast and his arms bound behind him.

Jessica gasped.

Derrick was right behind Matt. He looked defiant, but his arms were behind his back as well.

Chris followed them inside, his gun pointed at them.

They'd been captured.

Hope shattered around Jessica like a fragile vase being dropped on concrete.

"Where's Jeff?" Emily whispered, her tone frantic with worry.

Jessica shifted her eyes to Emily. Where *was* Jeff? Had he been killed?

Heart in her throat—if they'd killed Jeff, would Matt and Derrick be next?—her gaze shot to her children. What would these men do to them? To Emily? To her?

Stomach roiling with terror, she turned her attention to Matt, trying to catch his eye, but he stubbornly stared at the ground like he'd already been defeated.

"Another of their group is in the area," Chris said to the four men holding them captive, then he gestured to two of the men. "Find him and bring him here."

"Jeff," Emily whispered.

"Yes, sir," both men said before heading out the door.

If Jeff was still out there, maybe all hope wasn't lost.

Chris focused on the two remaining men. "Any progress here, Nate?"

Nate, the man Jessica thought was in charge, shook his head. "She," Nate pointed at Jessica, "refused to tell me where the keys are." He grinned. "Even after I roughed her up."

That's when Matt finally looked at her. Even though her cheek still throbbed from where Nate had slapped her, she tried to smile to show she was okay. Matt smiled back, but she could tell he was livid. He shifted on his feet like he was doing all within his power to keep from striking Nate.

Don't do it, don't do it she chanted in her head, terrified that if Matt tried to retaliate he would get hurt or worse.

When Chris nodded like he approved of Nate's methods, Jessica's fear notched up several levels. What were they capable of?

"Now that these men have been captured," Chris said with a glance at Matt and Derrick, "maybe we'll get somewhere." He grinned at Nate. "Take this one," he gestured with his thumb toward Derrick. "Somewhere private and have a little talk with him. Todd and I will chat with Matt." Chris's grin turned into a smirk. "He's the owner of this lovely RV."

A smile of anticipation curved Nate's lips. "Works for me." He grabbed Derrick by the upper arm and led him to a corner of the barn out of Jessica's view. She was surprised Derrick hadn't resisted. It seemed out of character for him. But when Chris and Todd each took Matt by an arm and practically dragged him in the other direction, she forgot about Derrick.

"Matt!"

He looked at her over his shoulder and gave her a reassuring smile. But she wasn't reassured. Not when both of those men were going to no doubt beat him until he gave them the key to his truck.

Dread clogged her throat, and when she looked at her children, who looked more frightened than she felt, she forced aside her distress and focused on them. "It's going to be okay," she whispered. "Dad will give them what they want and they won't hurt him."

Eyes wet with tears, Kayla nodded. Dylan looked angry and Cleo alternated between whimpering and barking. Emily, on the other hand, looked determined, like she believed Jeff would save the day. Jessica desperately hoped she was right.

A man cried out from the direction Matt had gone. Tears flooded Jessica's eyes. The thought of her sweet husband being hurt devastated her.

Derrick appeared, alone. Then Matt and Chris walked into view. Matt looked unharmed. He was even smiling. Confused, Jessica stared, her mouth hanging open. Matt hurried to her and wrapped her in his arms. After a long embrace, he pulled away and cradled her face in his hands. "Does it hurt?" In the confusion, she'd forgotten about her throbbing cheek.

"A little."

Chris came up behind Matt and said, "I'll be back in a few."

"What's going on?" she asked.

Matt grinned as he cut the zip ties from Jessica's hands, then he cut the zip ties from Kayla and Dylan and Emily's hands. "Chris is with us now." He glanced at Derrick, who ejected the magazine out of a gun he was holding, looked inside the magazine, then reinserted it. "Derrick and I weren't really tied up. It was a ruse."

Overwhelmed with happiness, she smiled. Then she remembered Brooke. "Brooke's missing."

Matt helped her stand. "Brooke's fine. She's the one who told us what had happened."

Jessica nearly staggered with relief.

"What about Jeff?" Emily asked as she stood.

"He probably disabled those other two men when they came out the door. That's what Chris is checking on."

"What did you and Chris do to that man?" Jessica asked. Though she didn't like the idea of them hurting him, what else could they have done?

"He's, uh, going to take a long nap."

She didn't want to know anything else. The important thing was they were safe. For now. "Is anyone else from the co-op going to come?"

Matt glanced at Derrick, who said, "Don't know."

That wasn't good enough. She hated the unknown. "Does Chris know?"

Derrick shook his head. "He didn't even know about the barn until we told him. Sounds like Russ and Eric didn't keep him completely in the loop."

A fresh spark of fear lit within her. "What if Russ and Eric come here?"

Matt put his arm around her. "They're dead."

Her eyes went wide. "Dead?! When? How?"

"At our house. Which is burning to the ground as we speak."

Even though she'd heard Matt report on the walkie that their house was in danger of being burned down, knowing the men of the co-op had succeeded tore a hole of sadness right through her heart.

"They burned our house down?" Kayla asked as her face crumpled.

"Derrick and Jeff's too," Matt said.

What was wrong with these people?

Chris came back into the barn followed by Jeff and Brooke.

Jessica ran to Brooke and threw her arms around her. In the short time she'd been with them, she'd come to feel like another daughter. Jessica pulled away and smiled softly at her. "I'm so glad you're all right."

Brooke smiled brightly. "Me too. When I saw those men going into the barn, I was so scared."

"But you found Matt and the others and told them what had happened." Warmth and appreciation for Brooke swept over Jessica. "If you hadn't done that..." She shook her head. "You saved us, Brooke."

Brooke beamed. "Just like you saved me."

Jessica hugged her again.

Cleo was prancing around bedside Brooke, who drew away from Jessica and knelt beside her dog, hugging her.

Kayla and Dylan joined Jessica and Brooke.

"Mom," Dylan said, "if our house is gone, where are we going to live?"

She put an arm around his shoulder. "It's just a building, Dylan. The important thing is that we're all okay."

Brooke stood from hugging Cleo. "You could move into my house."

"Uh, guys," Jeff said, coming to stand near them, Emily at his side. "We have a problem."

CHAPTER 45

Matt

Their plan had gone off without a hitch. They should be good to go. What was the problem now? Matt turned to Jeff with a frown. "What's wrong?"

Derrick and Chris joined the loosely formed circle.

Jeff's gaze swept over each of them, stopping on Chris. "When I was waiting for your two men to come out of the barn—"

"They're not my men," Chris said with a frown, interrupting him.

Jeff shook his head and sighed. "Regardless, I overheard them talking about how long it would be until the rest of their group could move in and take over the neighborhood. As you can imagine, I was curious to know what they were talking about, so when I, uh, incapacitated them, I decided it would be a good time to get more information." One side of his mouth quirked up like he'd enjoyed this task.

"What'd you find out?" Derrick asked.

"Evidently," Jeff said, his expression going deadly serious, "they belong to one of those gangs we've heard about. The ones who kill with impunity." He shook his head in disgust. "Those two moved into empty houses and pretended to be the residents. When the cooperative started up, they were right there supporting it, happy to help, happy to set the rules."

All eyes shifted to Chris, who shook his head. "Honestly, I didn't know half the guys who were part of the co-op so I can absolutely see them getting away with it."

Matt found that alarming. Who knew how many members of the co-op were legit and how many were outsiders? "Why'd they bother? I mean, why not just take what they want and leave?"

"They said they were looking for a place to settle their families. Somewhere they could eventually take over. When the cooperative was formed they offered their services in exchange for food." He swept his hands together. "Problem solved. For them."

"So," Derrick said with a disgusted snort, "what you're telling us is that an entire gang is preparing to move in to our neighborhood?"

Jeff said, "It's worse than that. Over the last couple of days most of their gang has *already* moved in to abandoned houses in our neighborhood." He grimaced. "They're here now and they won't leave without a fight."

"How many men are we talking about?" Chris asked.

Jeff pursed his lips. "At least twenty."

Deeply troubled, Matt considered the implications. If twenty gang members and their families had moved in, presumably in need of food, living in this neighborhood would be extremely dangerous. Especially now that word had gotten out that the Bronson's had food. After what they'd gone through that night, he had no desire to face violent gang members.

"Now that you mention it," Chris said, his forehead furrowed, "a few of my men—ones I know are legit neighbors—reported seeing a few unfamiliar faces over the last day or two. We were planning on paying them a visit when all the crap with Matt and his family took precedence." He frowned at Matt. "I'm still really sorry about what happened. It was all kinds of wrong."

Ready to move past that—Chris had more than proved he was on their side—Matt smiled. "It's all good."

"So, now what?" Jessica asked, fear plain in her eyes.

"We bug out," Derrick said, his expression set.

Everyone was quiet.

Jessica touched Matt's arm. He turned to her. Worry etched deep lines in her forehead. "Where will we go?"

That was a good question. They had their RV, which would allow them to go anywhere, but they needed a place to land.

Matt looked at Derrick and Jeff, who'd known each other before the crap had hit the fan. If they had a place in mind, that didn't help him. Yes, he'd been on the same team as them, but that didn't automatically mean he and his family were invited to wherever they were going—if they even had a place to go. His gaze switched to Chris. He had a wife and two small children, and from what Chris had said, they were about out of food. What were they going to do? Stay here? Word would get out that Chris had double-crossed the cooperative. That would be the end of them getting food from the co-op. And with the gangs moving in, it wouldn't be safe for anyone.

Matt didn't want to poke his nose where it wasn't wanted, but he had to ask. He turned to Derrick and Jeff. "Just curious. Do you have a place you're headed?"

Jeff and Emily grinned at each other, then turned to him with a smile. "Yeah. We do."

Nice for them, but it wouldn't do Matt or his family any good.

"My aunt and uncle have a spread in the San Joaquin Valley," Emily said.

"Where's that?" Dylan asked.

"Central California," Emily said as she turned to him. "The soil is rich there. Lots of agriculture."

Surprised they were willing to travel so far, Matt said, "That's a long way to go."

One side of Jeff's mouth tugged up, "Yeah. Like, seven hundred miles."

Going so far in today's world seemed insane, but if that's what they wanted to do, more power to them.

Derrick's eyebrows shot up. "You sure you want to do that?"

Jeff chuckled, then looked at Emily before facing Matt, Jessica, Derrick, and Chris. "Actually, we were hoping all of you would come with us."

"What?" Chris asked.

Matt looked at Jessica to see her reaction. She seemed uncertain. Smiling softly, he said, "Where else can we go?"

Fear filled her eyes once again. "I don't know."

Emily put an arm around Jessica. "You'll love it there. Best of all, no snow."

Jessica looked from Emily to Matt and back again. "I don't mind the snow."

"When we have a working furnace," Matt said, thrilled to think one of his worries could be resolved.

"But the trip..." Anxiety flashed in Jessica's eyes. "Won't it be dangerous?"

Yeah. It would. But did Matt want to confirm that? No. But he didn't want to give her a false sense of safety either. "You know what they say. It may not be easy, but it will be worth it. Besides, we won't be alone." He glanced at the other men. "Right?"

Jeff looked at Derrick and Chris.

Grinning, Derrick said, "Count me in."

That alone sent a burst of relief through Matt.

"I'd have to check with Amy," Chris said, "but it sounds like a good place to go."

"Hold on," Matt said as he thought of something else. He turned to Emily. "Do you think your aunt and uncle will be okay with you bringing all of us?"

She smiled. "I'm sure they'll be fine with it."

That sounded less certain. "When was the last time you talked to them?"

She looked at Jeff before facing Matt. "About a week and a half ago, I guess. They were worried about the way things were unfolding and invited us to come out. Things spiraled out of control before we could head out there, of course. So I know they'd be thrilled to have us." She smiled. "All of us."

Good enough. He looked at Dylan, Kayla, and Brooke. They would be in as much danger as the rest of them. They should have some say. "What do you guys think?"

Kayla and Brooke looked at each other, then at Matt. Smiling tentatively, Kayla said, "I don't really want to leave, but I know we have to. So, yeah. Let's do it."

Brooke nodded in agreement.

Proud of Kayla and Brooke for their willingness to go along with the plan, he smiled, then looked at Dylan.

"Yeah," he said without hesitation. "I'll go."

Matt raised his eyebrows at Jessica, who nodded with a tentative smile, then he turned to Emily and Jeff. "Looks like we're going."

Emily smiled. "Awesome."

"We'll leave at first light," Derrick said. "No reason to venture into the unknown in the dark."

Jeff nodded. "I agree. We'll sleep here tonight and take turns keeping watch."

"Hang on," Jessica said.

Everyone looked at her.

"I think we need to warn our neighbors—our *real* neighbors—about the gang members. Give them a chance to get out before things turn ugly."

Heads nodded all around.

"Anyone have an idea of the best way to do that?" Matt asked.

Chris held up a finger. "I need to head home and talk to my wife about leaving. On my way, I'll talk to a few men I trust and give them the word. They'll pass the message around to the right people."

That made Matt feel better. "Sounds good."

"Okay," Chris said, "I'll be back soon with my family."

Jeff clapped Chris on the back. "Glad to have you on board."

Chris smiled. "Thanks. I appreciate all of you making me part of your group despite, well, despite everything."

No one said anything, just nodded.

At that, Chris slipped out the rear door.

CHAPTER 46

Matt

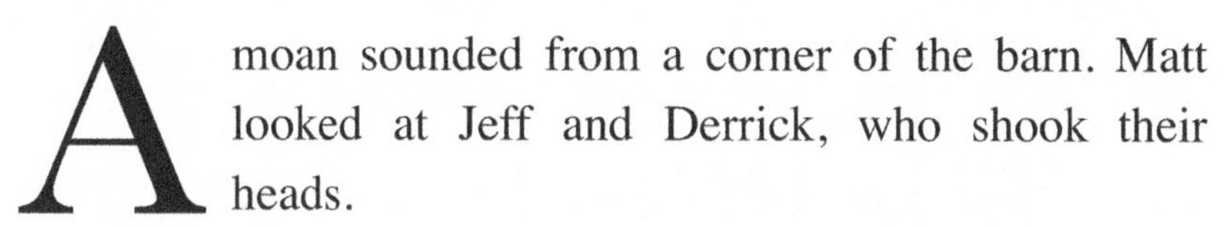

A moan sounded from a corner of the barn. Matt looked at Jeff and Derrick, who shook their heads.

"Someone's waking up," Derrick said with a smirk.

Matt had forgotten about the man they'd knocked unconscious. The man Derrick had taken care of would be waking soon as well. He turned to Jeff. "Do we need to, uh, worry about the men you talked to?"

With a grim expression, Jeff shook his head. "They won't be causing any more trouble."

Derrick and Matt brought the two men—Nate and Todd—into the main space. After making sure their hands and feet were firmly bound, and after slapping duct tape over their mouths, they secured them to a post in the barn.

"That ought to hold them," Derrick said.

Frowning, Jeff said, "We'll have to guard them tonight."

"Better to guard the known than guard against the unknown," Derrick said. "We'll leave them here when we take off tomorrow."

Matt agreed with Derrick. It would be a pain to have to guard these men as well as patrol around the barn, but if their group left in the dark, how far would they get? Would they be forced to stop in a dangerous place? Better to face that in the light of day.

Matt helped his family get settled in the RV for the night, then he took Cleo and offered to do first watch around the outside of the barn.

"Sounds good," Derrick said.

Matt held Cleo's leash and headed outside. He hoped having Cleo would give him an advantage. She would hear someone approaching way before he did.

An hour later, as he rounded the corner of the barn, Cleo began barking. Startled—Matt had hoped he wouldn't have to face more bad guys that night—he strained to see in the dark, focused on the direction Cleo was barking in.

"It's Chris," a voice called out.

Shoulders sagging in relief, Matt said, "Over here."

Chris came into view. He was alone.

"Where's your family?"

Chris smiled. "Waiting for me in the car. I wanted to check in before pulling up in my SUV. Didn't want to get shot at."

Matt grinned. "Good move." He paused. "So, you talked your wife into coming?"

Chuckling, Chris said, "Yeah. It wasn't easy. But she understands it's what's best for our family."

Matt nodded. "Exactly."

Chris jogged off while Matt went into the barn to tell Jeff and Derrick that Chris had arrived. Derrick was sleeping in his truck just outside the barn doors, but Jeff helped guide Chris as he backed into a spot beside Derrick's truck.

Matt finished his shift without incident, then he climbed into the RV, exhausted.

Curled up next to Jessica in their bed, Matt wondered where they would be when they next slept.

Early the next morning, a knock on the RV door woke Matt. He leapt from bed and hurried to the door.

Derrick stood on the other side. "We need to take care of a few things before we leave."

Matt nodded, then woke his family. The entire group gathered around Derrick.

"I've been thinking, and, unfortunately, your RV will be a huge target on this trek. I suggest we distribute your food and supplies among all the vehicles in case we lose the RV. That way we'll still have the bulk of your food."

They were a team so he didn't mind giving a large portion of it to them to carry. Besides, it made sense. "All right."

With everyone's help, they spread the food and other critical supplies among the four vehicles. Once they were satisfied, they climbed in their vehicles and left the barn. The sun was just beginning to light the day, fiery orange and red streaks filling the sky. It was a gorgeous sunrise and it gave Matt hope. They were headed on an adventure, one that would no doubt be fraught with danger, but one that would lead to a better life.

Glancing at Derrick's truck in front of him, and Jeff and Emily's truck and Chris's SUV behind him, Matt knew their group was strong. He wouldn't want to make this trek with anyone else. Sure, they would have their challenges, but they would stick together, protect each other. They were a family of sorts, one that could count on each other. In this crazy new world, family was the most important thing anyone could have. He meant to treasure his and do whatever he could to keep them safe.

Thank you for reading Pandemic: The Beginning. The story continues in Forced Exodus.

ABOUT THE AUTHOR

Christine has always loved to read, but enjoys writing suspenseful novels as well. She has her own eReader and is not embarrassed to admit that she is a book hoarder. One of Christine's favorite activities is to go camping with her family and read, read, read while enjoying the beauty of nature.

I love to hear from my readers. You can contact me in any of the following ways:

www.christinekersey.com
christine@christinekersey.com

Made in United States
North Haven, CT
06 September 2022